# Vital Era

## By Ann Riley

# Chapter 1

**Golden Sierra School August 7, 2090 – 9:15 a.m.**

The first day of school is a terrible time to be a teenager, especially when registered for high school. This terrible feeling filled most of the students walking into Golden Sierra School. Each of them dreading it, while carrying a suitcase for the school year.

The school was big and housed many things in its walls. It looked like a pharmaceutical corporation, with square buildings and a glass bridge connecting the two main buildings on campus. The school's unfriendly exterior caused many of its students to groan.

Several vehicles stopped in front of the unwelcoming buildings to let the weary students out to look at their home for the next school year. A white SUV idled at the curb, as a young woman and young boy got out. The siblings each had a look of dismay at returning to the school. They were both dressed in the school's uniform. The young woman wore a dark blue dress suit, while the boy wore a dark blue suit. The color of the uniforms went well with their caramel skin tone. They went to the back of the SUV and opened the trunk to grab their suitcases.

"Do you think Kay is already here?" the boy asked.

Vital Era

A Dragon Philosopher book.
Published through Kindle Direct Publishing.  Fourth addition.

www.dragonphilosopher.com

ISBN: 978-1-7328874-0-4

First addition Oct. 2017

Special thanks to my proof reader and editors B. Z. Smith, Sherrie Olson, and Steve Olson.  Couldn't have done any of this without them.

Cover produced by Dragon Philosopher team.

DRAGON PHILOSOPHER
TALES TO BE TOLD
www.dragonphilosopher.com

"Most likely, her parents probably dropped her off a day early," the young woman answered.

She fixed a strand of her honey brown hair back into the French twist on the back of her head.  With her hair pulled back into the French twist, her face looked like someone who was a bookworm, or at least that was what her brother had told her, after he said that, she had informed him that his face looked like an English prince to her.

"Do you have everything Will?" the young woman asked.

"Yes, I think so," he dragged his suitcase to the curb as he ran his hand over his crew cut light brown hair.

The young woman grabbed her suitcase and walked up to the passenger window.  The window rolled down so the driver could talk to her.

"Do you have everything Mabella?" the driver asked.

"Yes we do, you can leave now," she answered.

The driver nodded and drove the SUV away from the school and back to the road.

"Mabel, do you think this new school year will be a good one?" Will looked up at the cold buildings.

Mabel walked up next to him, "well it could be, but it could also be worse. Hopefully, Kay was able to keep up connections with Codie and his group, or we will be starting at square one."

Will looked at his sister and gave her a confused look, "that wasn't comforting."

Mabel shrugged her shoulders, "I wasn't trying to be comforting, but you don't need to worry. If Kay hasn't been successful, we can fix it."

Will grabbed Mabel's hand, "now that was comforting. Thank you."

Mabel smiled at him, "good, that time I was trying."

The two of them started walking towards the cold buildings.

**School Gym - 9:30 a.m.**

The gym sparkled like it was being prepared for royalty to walk across it. Gray hardwood floors shimmered from the bottom, and dark gray walls contained the room, with two basketball hoops hanging in the ceiling waiting to come down and play. The ceiling had several beams supporting it, making it look like a metal spider web.

Mabel and Will walked into the gym of the school with several hundred other students carrying their suitcases. Everyone seemed to be looking for their friends, including the siblings but their view had better insight to where their friend would be as they walked across the gym.

"There's Kay, sitting at the side," Will pointed to the bleachers with the kids on them.

Mabel followed his finger and saw Kay sitting on the front row corner on the side with her suitcase between her legs. Her burgundy hair was in pigtails, and wearing the blue dress suit made her skin look paler, but her muscular build made people whisper instead of tease her.

Will led the way to her, as they worked their way through the crowd. She looked up at them and gave them an annoyed look. Will had compared her face to a warrior about to throw food at the enemy.

"Hey Will and Mabel, you know how stupid it is that we are all trying to squish in here," Kay greeted them.

Will sat down beside her, and Mabel sat down next to Will.

"Did someone touch you or something?" Mabel asked.

"Yeah, I almost had to bite them," Kay responded.

"Really?" Will asked.

Kay gave Will a sarcastic look, "yes."

"Settle down students," a loud voice over a speaker system yelled into the gym causing the crowd to become quiet and making the students settle down on the bleachers in a matter of seconds.

In the center of the room stood a small podium with a woman standing at it speaking into the microphone. She wore a gray dress suit like the students' uniforms, which complemented her olive skin tone and her spiky dark gray hair. She looked at her audience like she held them captive, and most of the students' felt that way, because of her position of being principal.

"This week we start school students, and I would like to say a few words," she announced.

Kay leaned over to Will and Mabel, "I wonder if Principal Denzil remembers us?"

"Last year we had a few troublemakers that made it harder for the rest of us," Denzil continued.

"I think she remembers," Mabel whispered back.

"Let's try for a better year so we can all succeed and do our best for the future," Denzil looked over at Kay, Will, and Mabel.

"That felt like a personal remark," Will whispered.

"It was," Kay commented.

"Now students go to your dorms and get ready for tomorrow's classes; we are going to start this year off right," Denzil announced.

The crowd of students burst from their quiet cocoons and continued their conversations that had been going on before.

"At least she didn't mention us by name," Kay pointed out.

**Girls' Dorm – 10:04 a.m.**

Entering the building reminded most people of a doctor's office. With the girls going through a wooden door, down a white hallway, and passing black doors along the walls. The rooms behind the black doors held two beds, two desks, and two closets for two students. Mabel and Kay walked through one of the black doors while the other girls filed down the hallway like prisoners in jail going back to their cell.

"Hope Will has a good roommate this year," Mabel mumbled.

"Don't worry about it May, I got into the records of the school last night and gave him one of the most over-achieving students of our school, so he shouldn't have any trouble," Kay answered Mabel's quiet question.

"Thank you for doing that," Mabel placed her suitcase on her bed and opened it.

Kay kicked her bag under the other bed and fell onto the cold sheets, "I hate waiting."

Mabel gave her an amused look as she unpacked her clothes. She opened the closet on her side and started hanging up her belongings.

"Well, we could mess with some of the new students this year," Mabel suggested.

Kay rolled over and watched Mabel unpack, "you don't enjoy doing that, only I do. Besides, that isn't as fun anymore."

Kay sighed and sat up. She straightened her pigtails, as a knock at the door caught their attention.

"Enter!" Kay yelled.

The door opened as a young girl walked in, she looked confused and on the verge of tears.

"I was wondering if you could help me find a teacher?" she whispered.

Mabel stopped putting her stuff away, "what's wrong?"

The little girl looked at both of them, "one of the older girls took my bag and won't give it back to me."

"I'll take care of it," Mabel answered, as she walked to the door.

"Hey May, be careful. Remember we don't want attention tonight," Kay warned as she laid back down on her bed.

"I know, now show me where the girls are," Mabel ordered.

The girl led Mabel to a room five doors down and pointed at the door. Mabel went up and opened the door. In the room were four other girls, they were younger than Mabel but still older than the one they were bullying. They had a suitcase in the middle of the floor open, with its stuff all around the room.

"Okay, who's in trouble?" Mabel asked the room.

Three of the girls looked up in fear, while the fourth gave Mabel a snarky look.

"What are you? The snitch?" the girl asked.

Mabel noticed she was bigger than the others, making her appear more intimidating.

"Oh dear child, I'm worse than a snitch," Mabel smiled at the girl, "I'm the one who can beat you up and leave no mark."

Mabel seemed to fill the doorway as the other girls started filling the suitcase back up with its items. The snarky girl looked at them with disgust and stood up from the desk. She walked over to Mabel. But before she could speak Mabel punched her in the throat. The girl wheezed falling over from the impact, as the other girls gave her the suitcase.

"Next time this happens, all of you will be on the floor," Mabel warned.

### Seagull Drive, August 8, 2090 – 12:48 a.m.

The Golden Sierra School grew more menacing as darkness covered it, with very few lights from within to make the scene look any better. Those students that were new felt scared of what might prowl in the school's darkened hallways. But Mabel, Kay, and Will didn't fear the darkness, for they used it as a shield to escape the confining walls.

The trio walked out of the back door of the students' common room and into the night air. They had changed their clothes from their school's uniform to their street clothes. Mabel wore a plain black t-shirt with dark jeans and sneakers. Kay wore a blue button-up shirt open to a white undershirt and black leggings. And finally, Will had changed into a white t-shirt with a brown sports jacket and brown dress pants to match.

"So where's our bike?" Mabel asked as they walked to the street where that very morning they had been dropped off.

The street lights lit up orange circles of light along the road. Casting deep shadows upon the buildings down the street. The empty road gave a feeling of caution to those going down the eerie path.

"No bike," Kay answered.

Will and Mabel stopped at the sidewalk and gave Kay an annoyed look.

"How will we get to the games?" Will asked.

"What are we going to do, fly Kayleigh? I mean come on it's not like we can call a cab. The driver will know we are sneaking out from the school and most likely turn us in," Mabel complained.

"Well, our space for hiding the bike last year has been corrupted. It's now used to store textbooks and other junk. But I was able to a hide a scooter across the street in the for sale house," Kay pointed over the pavement towards the building opposite the school.

"The old Ridder Mansion?" Mabel asked.

"Yeah it's the only place to put stuff, and I doubt anyone is going to buy it," Kay walked across the street with the others following close behind.

"Why?" Will asked.

"Because the price for this ruined mansion is like over a hundred million dollars, and no one wants to spend that type of money on something so pathetic," Kay explained.

The trio walked on the cracked cement of the mansion's driveway and turned to the wall at the entrance. Kay walked over to an object hidden under an old blanket and pulled it off. Underneath it was a red motorized scooter.

Mabel looked at it funny, "how are we suppose to fit on that?"

Kay gave her a funny look back, "with a little effort of course."

**Cashe Corner – 1:05 a.m.**

The three of them held on to each other as Kay rode the scooter through the city. They went down dark alleys and behind buildings so no one would notice them while on the scooter.

"Has Codie been in Cashe Corner a lot?" Mabel asked she hung on to Will who sat between the two girls.

The wind tugged at them as they traveled down another empty street behind old buildings. The Cashe Corner district had old buildings making up the area, which made it not match the name. Nothing new seemed to fit in, and most people stayed in at night, so not to get caught up in any trouble.

"Yeah, there's been trouble in other parts of the city, and he wants to stay away from it," Kay told them.

"Anything we should be worried about?" Mabel looked over her shoulder as an alley cat ran the other direction.

"Right now it's just rumored, when it becomes gossip then we worry," Kay answered.

"What about our container?" Will asked.

Kay rode around a garbage pile, "they all got moved here after the Knight team got taken down."

"What!?" Mabel and Will yelled in unison.

Kay slowed the scooter down as they turned a corner, "yeah it was weird. The police came out of nowhere and surprised our community."

"Did any of them get hurt?" Will looked concerned.

"No, it wasn't that bad. The team got released, but the Draconis can't let them in because they got caught," Kay stopped the scooter and looked out at the main road.

She looked both ways before turning on to it and going down the road.

"How'd the team take it?" Mabel's face became serious.

"They broke up," Kay answered, as they sped away, "they didn't have a reason to be a team anymore."

"It's a good thing you live here Kay," Will pointed out, "or we would be in the dark about this."

"Yeah it is," Mabel looked up at the dark sky, "so did you make any money while we were gone?"

Kay chuckled, "don't worry. We will be able to pick up where we left off. Our container has stayed in check, and we still have good connections."

Kay stopped the scooter at a red light. The trio watched the light waiting for it to turn green.

"Has anyone hacked the traffic lights yet?" Mabel laughed a little at her question.

"No, and Codie has claimed it to be illegal among us," Kay looked over her shoulder at them, "that's what got the Knight team taken down. They had been the ones trying to hack the system but failed to realize how strong this city is. The police tracked them down through their efforts to get in."

Will stared at Kay in fear, "I hope Codie doesn't ask us to do anything like that."

"Oh don't worry," Mabel looked back up at the sky, "I'm going to ask him."

# Chapter 2

Kay stopped the scooter, and the three of them looked at Petal Junkyard. Due to the recent increase in traffic to the junkyard, a lot of its content had been removed or placed on the perimeter to form a wall around the area. The old junkyard had been cleaned from years of being piled with garbage. Kay, Mabel, and Will got off the scooter. Kay pushed it as they walked into the junkyard. Entering the yard gave way to a small community within. Old shipping containers lined a small dirt road down the middle with three levels of containers stacked on each other with rope ladders to the second and third levels.

"It stinks," Mabel commented.

"Don't worry, the smell's not strong, and you'll get use to it," Kay informed her two friends.

People walked around the busy road, as the trio started making their way down the dirt road. The area felt like a mid-day marketplace instead of the middle of the night in a garbage dump. Everyone seemed to have a feeling of excitement about them. It made for an intoxicating atmosphere that drew people in.

The trio walked around a group of people arguing about a broken motorcycle on the road.

"Well, it looks like everyone is here," Will pointed out.

"Hey the Vital Era team is back," a young woman in front of the trio called.

She walked up to the group with another woman.

"Hey Nelly and Debbie, how have the Soldiers been?" Mabel greeted them.

Nelly, wore a gray sweater jacket with a red and black striped skirt. Her skin seemed to glow like honey, which emphasized her straight lavender hair.

"We're good, been missing the care your team brings to the playing field," Nelly said.

Debbie wore short jeans and a pink hoody. Her short orange-red hair looked like fire compared to her chocolate skin tone. She hugged Will and Mabel at the same time.

"Hey Debbie," Will said happily.

"How has your summer been?" Mabel asked as Debbie released her embrace on the two siblings.

"Good, we took home a few hearts and were able to take home even better loot," Debbie gave them her best smile.

"Yeah made a couple of teams look bad from what I can remember," Kay leaned on the red scooter as they talked.

"Someone has to keep these people in line," Nelly chuckled.

"How have you two been holding up?" Debbie asked.

Mabel and Will exchanged a look between themselves before answering.

"We were bored out of our minds," Will commented.

Kay gave them each a curious look before speaking, "well I need to show these two where our container is now, we'll see you later."

The two women nodded their heads and headed off in another direction. Kay looked back at her two teammates and gave them another curious look.

"Bored out of your minds. Is that how you describe losing your mother to someone?" Kay asked.

Mabel shook her head and started pushing the scooter, making Kay stand up.

"It's not like it was unexpected," Will whispered.

**Vital Era Container – 1:26 a.m.**

Kay led the group down the dirt road until they stopped in front of a container in the lineup of mismatched colored shipping containers. She walked up to the green one and took out a key from her pocket for the padlock on the latch.

Will looked at the other two containers on top of their own, "who's our neighbors?"

"The Soldiers, and the Magic," Kay answered.

Kay took the padlock off the door and opened the rusted latch. The hinges squeaked as the doors swung open. In the old green container, there were tables, tools, and mechanical parts everywhere. There was a cot at the back along with two laptops sitting on it and three chairs along with two tables with lamps to the side filling the container. A big chest was hidden under the cot.

"It looks good Kay, but how did you manage to get a bottom spot," Mabel leaned against the frame and gave Kay a suspicious look.

Will walked pass the girls and over to one of the laptops on the bed.

"I know how to work it," Kay gave Mabel a suspicious look back.

"She begged for it," a woman's voice answered.

The trio turned to the new voice. A woman in her early twenties walked up to the group. She wore a yellow tank top and white sweatpants with black flower prints. Her golden blonde hair was braided, and her rich walnut skin tone shimmered in the lights coming from the top of the containers.

"Kassidy that isn't true," Kay protested.

Mabel shook hands with Kassidy, "Hey Kassidy Platt, I hear we're neighbors."

"Yeah," Kassidy nodded, and then pointed out to Kay, "right, but you didn't move from this spot until they placed your container here. What would you call that?"

Kay shook her head and stomped inside the container. Mabel watched her pout with an amused look.

Mabel turned back to Kassidy, "so how have you been?"

Kassidy shrugged her shoulders, "fine, but I did just meet some weird people."

Will perked up in curiosity, "weird for normal people, or weird for people who hang out in a junkyard?"

Kassidy smirked, "I would say for normal and junkyard people that they were weird. Two of them had bright yellow hair."

The trio gave her a strange look.

"A lot of people have dyed hair," Kay pointed out.

"Yeah, well most don't have matching bright yellow irises, and bodyguards with different colored hair and eyes," Kassidy explained to them.

The trio looked at each other then back to Kassidy, before bursting into laughter. Kassidy shook her head at them with a smile on her face.

"I said weird," Kassidy waved a hand at them, "see you later."

They waved back as she left.

"That's crazy," Kay grabbed her sides.

"Contacts hurt," Will sat down on the cot, "their eyes must be burning."

Mabel chuckled, "it is fascinating, but we need to get to business. Kay where is my bike?"

Kay still shook with laughter, "oh don't worry it's with the other bikes in the parking lot."

## Blue Bird Street – 2:32 a.m.

Looking at her watch, Kay announced, "a race between the Vikings, Spells, Seals, and Blacksmiths just barely started, do you guys want to go and watch."

Will looked up from the laptop, "that sounds nice."

Mabel stood up from a chair and stretched, "it will be good to get out of the container for a moment."

They all walked out of the container. Kay and Mabel pushed the doors closed, as Will placed the latch across them. Kay put the padlock on the latch locking it. The trio started walking down the road towards a loud commotion.

"What street is it on?" Will asked.

"Blue Bird," Kay answered.

They hurried out of the junkyard and down a block until they came to the street, a crowd already stood on the sidewalks watching the street. Pushing through the crazy crowd, they finally made it to the front. Three big monitors entertained everyone with videos from the four different teams competing in the race.

Cameras were mounted in the riders' helmets, and the crowd cheered as they watched the scenes unfold.

Four modified motorcycles rode through Palaco City's empty streets. The motorcycles were equal length to a car, and just as steady. The bikes had two thick tires with them extended out the front and back of the vehicle. The seat and steering were elevated above the tires. Each bike had two people on it with one driving and the other wielding a weapon.

The Viking group's bike was green with black tires. It cut in front of the other riders and continued down the street. The passenger on the bike carried a modified bow; they pulled back the string with no arrow. But a light filled the slot of the arrow, and the individual pointed it at another bike before releasing the light.

It shot across the area and hit the bike, disappearing once it made contact. The bike lost power, and the vehicle stopped in the street as the other three continued in the race.

"Wow, Blacksmiths are out!" someone yelled.

"Yeah, they didn't see that one coming!" another person chimed in.

The three bikes raced down the street, as the Blacksmiths camera was turned off. The crowd cheered as it continued.

"That's shocking!" Will said to Mabel and Kay.

"It is; Kay was this expected?" Mabel asked.

Kay nodded, "it's not as shocking as you might think, but it still is a great improvement for the Vikings."

The trio turned their attention back to the monitors. The Seals bike was completely black, and the passenger carried a rifle. The passenger loaded the gun and started firing bullets of light at the other bikes. The bullets were similar to the arrows being shot from the Vikings.

"They're almost here!" a man announced.

The crowd turned away from the screens and looked down the street. The bikes came rushing into view. Charging down the street, the fight between the Seals and Vikings was still going on. And they didn't see the Spells bike go around them and take the lead. Within seconds the bikes passed the street light at the end, and the crowd cheered as the race concluded.

**Spiral Parking Garage – 3:58 a.m.**

The five-story parking garage in Cashe Corner had seen better days like the rest of the area. It was called Spiral Parking and was still being used despite its old age. But the main use had shifted, now it housed the motorcycles of the junkyard people. And because of that, the security of the place had been increased to protect against cops and robbers. The giant gray structure was more comparable to a fort than a parking lot.

And at almost four in the morning, it sounded like a club, as loud music could be heard and lights could be seen within. Kay and Will leaned against one of the pillars on the fourth floor, as they watched a dance party rage in front of them.

"I never cared for dancing," Will commented.

"You shouldn't judge dancing on what you see here," Kay laughed, "these people can't dance."

Mabel walked around the jumping bodies with two armor suited people. When the armor was fully put on it made the viewer feel intimidated. The suit was electric and glowed with the power going over the body in the form of the lights looking like a circuit board. Their light was green, and the sleek silver exterior shimmered in the light. The helmet was completely black and was so clear that people could see their reflection in it. But the face of the person inside couldn't be seen. They stood like metal beings waiting to be served by the human race. The two of them had green fabric around the waist signifying their part of the Viking team.

Mabel shook their hands and walked away from them. She went over to Kay and Will, to lean against the pillar too.

"So," Kay looked to Mabel, "did you talk to Codie?"

Mabel shook her head, "couldn't find him."

"But don't worry I found you."

The trio turned around to see a man and a young woman standing behind them. The man, Codie, wore a blue t-shirt, jeans, and an old leather jacket. He had long curly dark ginger hair and toasted tan skin tone. He was average height and had a muscular build.

The young woman, Joi, a team member of Codie's group, wore a small black dress, with black leggings, and a purple silk jacket. She had frizzy electric blue hair, and her skin tone was beige. She was taller than Codie but had a slimmer build.

"Codie and Joi!" Will said shocked.

Codie walked up to the group and shook their hands, "don't act so surprise Wilt, I knew your team would look for me once you all got here."

"You can just call me Will," Will said, "no one uses my given name."

"Or he saw Mabel walking around looking for him," Joi said.

Codie punched her in the arm, "hey, don't ruin my mystery."

"Codie," Mabel interrupted the two, "I want to talk about the games."

**Seagull and Albatross Intersection – 4:38 a.m.**

Codie, Mabel, Kay, and Will stood at the Seagull and Albatross intersection. Joi had to take care of other things only Codie had followed the trio to the intersection. Kay had pushed their scooter from the Vital Era container to the area, and she and Will rested on it while Mabel talked to Codie. The small group looked like they were making a deal with an old fashion devil because of how the orange light splashed on them.

"If we make the Draconis games legal by going to the police and courthouse we can finally come out of the shadows," Mabel explained to him.

She was eager for Codie to understand her. But he shook his head.

"I don't know how that would be even possible Mabella," Codie placed a hand on her shoulder, "our relationship with the police and city is so bad that I don't think a conversation could be started with them."

Mabel nodded, "I understand that, and I'm not saying this is easy. But we defy the odds against us. Just look at what we achieve in the games.

Most people couldn't imagine what we do. And developing the games to what they are now was nearly impossible, but we did it. How is this any different?"

Codie released her shoulder and scratched his head, "Dear May, it's different because we have lives to lose now. When this was starting, yes it was nearly impossible, but all we had to lose back then were our lives. And during that time our lives weren't worth saving... Now we have families and friends and a community among ourselves. We can't lose that."

Mabel looked like she was losing an important game, "I know we have more to lose, but at the rate we are going, we will become criminals, and nothing will be able to save us."

Kay and Will looked at each other; they had never heard Mabel plea before. Codie looked her in the eyes and saw the fear she was hiding from her team. He nodded before speaking.

"I get why you're concern about this. And maybe your right. In our current situation we can pull out, but anything could happen. So I am permitting you to find a solution to the games illegalness."

Mabel lit up at his words.

"But if something goes wrong and you're caught. There will be nothing we can do for you or your team," Codie paused, "do you understand that your decision involves Kayleigh and Wilt and not just you."

"I go by Kay, not Kayleigh," Kay whispered.

Mabel agreed, "I understand, and I will talk to them about this."

Codie nodded again, "good, be seeing you later."

He waved at them before walking back towards the junkyard. The trio watched him go before talking among themselves.

"Well you got the permission you were looking for," Kay smirked at her.

Mabel turned to them, "I know the games mean a lot to us, but…"

Will jumped off the scooter and tackled Mabel to the ground, "don't worry Mabel we are with you on this."

Mabel hugged her little brother. The trio got onto the scooter and started driving back towards Golden Sierra School.

# Chapter 3

The lunchroom looked like the gym of Sierra School. It was light gray for the floorboards, and dark gray for the walls, the only thing different was the lineup of long white tables for the students to eat on. The room was full today with several students eating lunch.

Mabel sat in a section of a table; she was focused on her notebook that had a map of Palaco City. Her eyes searched it, looking for someplace to give them hope. Kay walked down one of the isles towards her with two lunch trays. Sitting down next to Mabel, Kay handed her a tray.

"Still can't find a place?" Kay asked she gave her misshapen food a disgusted look.

Mabel shook her head, "there aren't any good areas. This searching is pointless."

Will walked towards them quickly. He carried a tray of food also and placed it on the table as he sat down.

"Well, I just had a strange moment," Will said.

The girls gave Will their attention.

"What happened?" Mabel asked.

"Well, while I was in line getting my lunch, Hector came up to me," Will said, "and he was just about to take my food."

"Oh do I need to go and talk to him again," Mabel started to stand up.

"No," Will shook his head.

Mabel sat back down, as the girls continued to listen to him.

"My roommate Jericho stopped him," Will informed them.

Kay and Mabel shared a look between each other.

"Well, that was unexpected," Kay mumbled to herself and went back to poking at her food with a plastic fork.

"Yeah, I mean he was nice to me when he found he was going to be my roommate, but I didn't expect him to remember me outside of the room. He is a busy guy," Will gave his food a concerned look.

"Wilt!" a young man called.

The trio looked up and saw two boys walking up to the table. The older one of the two had slick black hair and a tan skin tone. The other boy's hair was shaggy golden brown and had a fairer skin tone. They both wore the school's uniform.

"Hey Jericho," Will greeted the older one, "you can call me Will."

Mabel thought to herself that Jericho had a face similar to a CEO she had seen and that the younger boy's face reminded her of a puppy.

"This is my brother Baylor," Jericho pointed to the young man, "we were wondering if you were alright after Hector stopped bugging you?"

The trio stared at the two of them. Shock covered their faces as they remained speechless. The two boys looked concerned at them.

"Are you three okay?" Baylor asked.

Before any of them could respond, a bell sounded throughout the school, and the trio slipped away from the other boys.

**Science Classroom – 12:45 p.m.**

The classrooms of Golden Sierra School were different in color to the lunchroom and gym, but not in feeling. The walls were dark orange, and the floor was white tile. In the science room, there were two rows of tables each with tall chairs waiting for the students. The students filed into the room.

Mabel and Kay sat down at a tall table, placing their backpacks next to the sink on it.

"That was strange," Kay commented, "I didn't think Jericho ever pulled his nose out of the book he was reading."

Students continued to file into the room, including Jericho and Baylor but the girls didn't see them come in until they walked up to their table.

"Hey," Jericho greeted.

The girls gave the boys a strange look again.

"I didn't mean to startle you back there," Jericho awkwardly scratched his head.

Mabel tilted her head, "he's still talking to us."

Kay shook her head, stood up, and walked to the front of the classroom where the teacher's station was.

"If we are bothering you we can leave," Baylor said, he looked concerned.

Mabel straightened her neck and rubbed her hands together, "well, we just find it strange that you would talk to us, or continue to talk to us."

"Why do you think that?" Jericho asked.

"You two don't talk to anyone," Mabel pointed out.

"We do talk," Baylor whispered.

The sprinklers on the ceiling sprang to life and sprinkled water across the classroom on the students. Screams and yells echoed as students raced out of the room. Smoke covered the teacher's station, but no fire burned. Mabel stayed calm as everyone ran out of the room, including Jericho and Baylor. She grabbed her bag and Kay's bag, before walking up to the smoking teacher's station.

"Was this necessary?" she asked.

Kay peeked from around the smoke, "hey they were acting unpredictable, I had to do something to get rid of them."

"We could have just asked them to leave," Mabel threw Kay her bag.

"Yeah, but then they would have been suspicious," Kay started walking towards the door.

"And causing a panic doesn't seem suspicious to you?" Mabel shook her head as she followed Kay out of the classroom.

Students were standing in the halls dripping wet, with most of them trying to get some of the water off. Mabel and Kay didn't mind the water that had sprinkled over them. They just continued their stroll out of the room and to the nearest bathroom to dry their clothes off.

Jericho and Baylor watched them calmly walk out of the room, as they twisted their clothes to get the water out.

"Well, they didn't seem to be in a hurry," Baylor pointed out.

"Yeah, you know the other night I swear I looked over at Will's bed and didn't see him there, and now his sister acts like this," Jericho shook his wet hair to get the water out, "something is going on…I hope it's not drugs."

**Ridder Mansion – 11:23 p.m.**

Walking across the street, the siblings and friend went up to the old mansion. They had street clothes on, Mabel in her black t-shirt, Kay wearing her blue button-up shirt, and Will in his brown sports jacket.

"Denzil still hasn't figured out what went wrong, but you and Kay are still being banned from science class," Will laughed, "I never seen you react like that Kay."

Mabel walked pass the Ridder Mansion wall, while Kay and Will stopped on the sidewalk to talk.

"They were pushy," Kay placed her hands on her hips, "you can't expect me not to freak-out!"

"They barely talked to us," Will smiled.

Mabel pushed the scooter out from behind the wall, but stopped after looking up, "we have a problem."

Kay and Will looked to her, as she pointed across the street. Jericho and Baylor jogged up to them. Jericho had a red collared shirt, and black pants on that made him look even more like a CEO. Baylor, on the other hand, looked like a librarian with a blue sweater shirt, and brown pants. The two of them stopped on the sidewalk next to Kay and Will.

"Please don't do this," Jericho placed his hands on the shoulders of Will and Kay.

Baylor looked at Mabel and gave her a comforting smile. Mabel gave him a crooked smile back.

"Okay," Will said, "now I see pushy."

"Yeah, now I think it's shifted to just creepy," Kay pushed his hand off of her shoulder.

"You guys don't have to go through with this," Jericho said.

Mabel placed the scooter on its kickstand and sat down on it, "what exactly do you think we are doing here?"

Jericho looked to Mabel, "running away after the fire incident."

The trio laughed at the brothers. Mabel went back to pushing the scooter to the street, pushing through the small group they had formed on the sidewalk.

"That's not what you're doing?" Jericho asked confused.

"Where did the scooter come from?" Baylor asked quietly.

"I bought the scooter at a garage sale a couple of weeks ago," Kay answered as she got on the vehicle.

Will got on the scooter next, then Mabel took her place on the seat.

"We aren't running away, and you don't need to worry about what we do in our spare time," Mabel gave them both a smile, "go back to studying. We would hate for you to fall behind."

Kay started the scooter and sped down the street, leaving the boys in the orange light of the street to watch them leave. Jericho walked into the middle of the road and scratched his head.

"I wish we could follow them," he murmured.

"We can," Baylor walked back across the street and Jericho followed, "just track their phones, like you do with everyone and I'll drive. There are dirt bikes from last year's obstacle course."

**Petal Junkyard, August 12, 2090 – 12:29 a.m.**

Baylor stopped the dirt bike as the brothers looked into Petal Junkyard. They were shocked at what they saw. The many people, small dirt road, and stacked containers made them question what was going on.

"This was surely unexpected," Baylor said.

"Hey, you guys," a muscular man with a Mohawk walked up to the brothers, "what are you looking at?"

"Um, we…were looking for some friends," Jericho explained, "I don't know if you have seen them. Mabella and Wilt Overton, along with Kayleigh Eldred?"

The man grabbed them both by the arm and yelled over his shoulder, "Spence go get the Vital Era team, and Jeff bring the dirt bike in. It seems we have rats sniffing around."

The man dragged the brothers into the junkyard as another man took their bike. A crowd formed around them as they were sat down on two hard chairs in front of a blue container.  The crowd of people watched the newcomers like they were spies sent to infiltrator them.

"We don't mean to be rude, but we're just here to see our friends," Jericho tried to explain again.

Codie walked through the crowd to the front and stared at the new captives.  Everyone's attention went to him, as he considered the brothers. Mabel pushed through the crowd and placed herself between Codie and the brothers.

"I can explain," Mabel said.

Codie gave her a sad look, "did they follow you from school?"

Kay and Will came to the front of the crowd and watched the scene unfold.

Mabel looked back at the brothers.  Their expression was shocked at the situation they had suddenly been pulled into.

"They're friends…we invited them to come with us, but they got lost…we were going to inform the Draconis council but weren't sure they were coming tonight," Mabel lied.

Codie's face became serious as he studied Mabel's eyes, "are you saying they are new members of your team Mabella?"

Kay and Will shook their heads no, but Mabel turned her gaze to the ground.

"Yes," she quietly said, "they are new members of Vital Era."

People in the crowd gasped at the news, and murmurs rippled through it.

"Mabella," Codie said sternly, "I'm going to ask you again, and I want you to think about why you should change your answer…Did they follow you from school?"

"No, they didn't follow us," Mabel straightened herself, "we are prepared to accept the consequence of adding new members to the team."

Codie shook his head and whispered to Mabel, "you don't have to do this. You could take the fine, and they would be taken care of."

Codie turned away from Mabel and the brothers and walked away.

**Draconis Container – 12:52 a.m.**

The trio and brothers followed Codie down the dirt road. A crowd still followed and talked among themselves, while Mabel and the others remained quiet. The brothers had stopped asking questions.

Codie led them to the last container on the road. It was a very old red one. Joi stood there waiting for them; she opened the container doors so they could walk in and closed the doors behind them so the crowd couldn't hear the conversation they were about to have.

The container had two lamps on an old metal desk. They illuminated the room, giving it an eerie vibe to those in it when closed off from the road. Codie sat down at the desk, while the trio and brothers remained standing. Mabel still stood between Codie and the others.

Codie looked up at them, "Mabella, this is very serious."

Mabel nodded, "I know."

Codie shook his head, "Keyleigh and Wilt, do you agree with Mabella's announcement that these two individuals are joining your team?"

Kay stepped up, "yes, we agree with her stupid announcement."

Will nodded.

Codie let out a sigh, "fine, do wish to pay or race for their entry into the Draconis games?"

"Why can't we just leave?" Jericho asked.

Codie let out another sigh, "either you join the Vital Era team, or we make sure you never talk about this to anyone."

"How would you do that?" Jericho asked again.

His brother gave him a funny look and shook his head at him, but Jericho ignored it.

"In a very cruel way," Codie answered seriously.

Baylor put a hand on Jericho's shoulder, and the older brother backed down from the questioning.

"How much would it cost to add them to the team?" Mabel asked.

"Ten thousand," Codie informed, "a person."

Will and Kay shared a look of concern between the two of them. Mabel rubbed the back of her neck.

"We'll race then," Mabel decided.

Will grabbed Mabel's hand, and Kay grabbed her shoulder.

"No," Will said.

"We don't need to do this, they aren't worth it," Kay warned.

Mabel looked over her shoulder at Kay, making her take her hand off. Codie watched the trio quietly, as did the brothers.

Codie nodded, "Mabel, we are racing tonight, and it's going to be a single rider because of the two boys."

"I understand," Mabel agreed.

"Go to your container, and suit up. Then take the brothers to the garage, where they will be given protective armor, okay?" Codie asked.

"Okay," Kay answered, before storming out of the container. Will slowly followed her. Mabel gave Codie one final look, before pulling the two brothers out of the container and down the dirt road.

# Chapter 4

**Spiral Garage August 12, 2090 – 1:25 a.m.**

Mabel, Kay, Will, Jericho, and Baylor stood on the first floor of the Spiral Garage. Mabel was suited with the electric armor. She held her black helmet in her hands as Kay got the signal with her phone from the camera inside the helmet. Mabel's armor looked like the other armor the teams had, but with a different color from the Vikings suit. The lights which looked like a circuit board glowed yellow. Will tied a yellow ribbon around Mabel's waist, signifying her part of the Vital Era team.

Jericho and Baylor watched the team get ready for the race.

"It looks like you are going to war," Baylor commented.

Mabel gave them a tired look, "in this community; it is like going to war. If I lose this race, we are going to owe the council double the amount of money."

"So forty thousand dollars!" Jericho exclaimed, "why didn't you pay the twenty thousand instead!"

Mabel shook her head at Jericho, "we don't have that type of money to spare."

"You could have let them take the fall," Kay whispered.

Mabel sighed, "you know we couldn't do that to them."

Will finished tying the ribbon and started walking away, "you remember what happened to Barbara's boyfriend. That was harsh."

Will walked over to a big gray tarp and pulled it off. Underneath it was one of the modified motorcycles. It stood tall, Will's chest came up to the seat, with its two thick tires and elevated seat and motor. Will released the break, and pushed it up to Mabel.

"Is that a motorcycle?" Jericho asked.

"Well it's not a bird," Kay said snarkily.

"It's so big," Baylor went over to the bike and ran his hand along the seat.

"It has to be so more than one person can be on it at a time," Will informed them.

Mabel placed her helmet on the seat, before going over to Will and hugging him. He returned the hug. Mabel released him and walked over to Kay.

"I'm not hugging you," Kay pouted, "this could have been avoided."

Mabel sighed before embracing her, and Kay returned the embrace stubbornly.

"What's going to happen?" Baylor asked.

Mabel released Kay, and turned her attention to the brothers, "you are going to be fitted with a helmet and chest piece of armor. You will be placed on a moving truck, where I and other racers will try to reach you, as the truck drives through the city."

"Then what?" Jericho inquired.

"The racers will try to pull you onto their motorcycle," Mabel answered.

"That's dangerous!" Jericho exclaimed.

Before anyone could speak, Codie and two other men walked up to the small group.

"It's time for you boys to get suited up, the race is going to start in fifteen minutes, Mabella. You better be ready," Codie warned.

The men grabbed the brothers by their shoulders and led them away. Codie followed after them.

**Kingfisher and Parrot Intersection – 1:41 a.m.**

Mabel pushed her bike along the road. People lined the street cheering. The other riders were in position at the start of the intersection. The Vikings bike was there, with their rider Jim already suited up for the race, and glowing green.

The Spells' rider connected her helmet on; her suit glowed blue. Debbie, the rider for the Soldiers team, watched Mabel push her bike next to hers. Debbie still held her helmet in her arms, as her suit glowed silver.

"You okay?" Debbie asked Mabel.

Mabel shook her head, and sat herself down on her bike, "I haven't raced for almost a year."

"Since the crash with the Knights team, right?" Debbie asked.

Mabel nodded, "yeah."

A man walked to the center of the road and started announcing the race.

"Tonight, we have four teams competing for the prize of two new teammates for the Vital Era!" the man yelled out, "or for twenty thousand dollars!"

The crowd cheered at the announcement.

Debbie shook her head, "I wish this part could be changed in the games. I hate it so much."

Mabel looked at Debbie, "you better give it your all. If anyone accuses you of favoritism, a fine will be placed on your team. And I will have to go through this all over again."

Debbie smirked, "don't worry about me, Mabel."

Debbie placed her helmet on and snapped it into place. She then revved her engine, making the crowd go wild. Mabel looked at the crowd searching it until her eyes found Kay and Will. They waved at her. She smiled and waved back.

"Because there are two new members on the team, there will only be the riders tonight," the man continued to announce, "so riders be ready to fight this battle on your own."

Mabel gave another sigh, before putting her helmet on and connecting it to the neck armor of her suit. With the connection, the helmet came alive and lite up on the inside. The shatterproof glass of her helmet became a screen that tracked the movement of the other motorcycles, and the possible path she could take. The screen used white light, to signify the information.

Mabel breathed heavily, as she heard the announcer introducing the teams. Her heart started to beat in her ears, causing other sounds to be lost from them.

"Okay," she whispered to herself, "time to race. I have to win this."

The announcer finished and walked off the street. Two women and one man took their place holding rags in the air. The other riders revved their engines as the countdown started.

"Three!" the crowd yelled.

Mabel took one more deep breath, before revving her bike.

"Two!"

The people holding the rags brought them down in a dramatic motion.

"One!" the crowd yelled once more.

**Cashe Corner – 2:03 a.m.**

During this time of night, Cashe Corner had very little traffic on the streets. So the motorcycles went down the street in quick blurs of light, without any traffic to worry about.

The sounds from the roaring engines blocked out her heart beat, as Mabel kept up pace with the other riders. Everything, but the bikes, blurred as they continued to pick up speed. They turned a corner sharply, causing all their tires to squeal and leave black marks on the asphalt.

"How are you doing Mabel?" Will asked over the communications in the helmet.

Mabel smiled to herself, "I'm doing great!"

She shifted gears and pulled ahead of the other riders.

"Girl, take it slow," Kay said, "don't be so reckless."

Mabel led the group of riders around a different turn and continued to hold the lead. The other riders formed into a tight pack around her as they went throughout the city.

"How are the other riders doing?" Mabel asked.

"They're keeping up with you," Will answered.

"But none of them have even come close to challenging you yet," Kay pointed out, "probably waiting to see if you will run yourself out before the race even starts."

Mabel turned another corner and swerved to avoid a parked car on the side of the road. The other riders made similar moves around the vehicle.

"Anything on the police scanners?" Mabel asked.

"Nope, it looks like we are in the clear tonight," Will answered.

"At least something has gone our way this night," Kay sighed, "you know we will probably have to sell the bike just to pay for this race."

The Spells rider, Barbara, increased her speed to match Mabels'. The two riders led the group now through the streets, with their yellow and blue lights streaking behind them.

"We aren't going to lose Kay," Mabel looked at Barbara.

The two riders stared at each other, even though their helmets prevented them from seeing each other's faces.

"Oh really?" Kay said sarcastically, "you haven't raced in like a year. Tell me how you're going to suddenly shake off those cobwebs and race like you never stopped."

"She practiced at our house," Will chimed in.

Mabel turned her attention back to the road. The motorcycles passed a bicycler on the road, causing a huge rush of air to knock her over.

"You didn't tell me you had practice over the summer," Kay remarked.

"We didn't want to get your hopes up, Kay. Mabel had been doing fine, but she still hadn't reached her standard of driving yet," Will explained.

"Well you better be happy with it now," Kay mumbled.

A red light flashed in Mabel's helmet. It was between the two white lights that guided her possible path.

"I just got the beacon for the truck," Mabel announced.

"The other riders got it too, get ready for the race to begin," Kay warned.

The other riders sped up to match Barbara and Mabel's bikes. The red light blinked several times before turning green and becoming solid. The motorcycles then roared out, as they finally had their destination.

**Freeway – 2:18 a.m.**

"I'm heading on to the freeway right now," Mabel informed Kay and Will.

The four motorcycles entered the freeway at a high velocity. They still rode in a tight cluster as they neared their destination. They were getting closer to the green dot.

The freeway had very few vehicles on the road at night, most of them were travelers trying to get home. Mabel avoided a minivan, as the bikes started to reach higher speeds. Sounds from the engines working overtime filled the air, with a smell of oil growing in stench.

Within a few moments, the bikes finally came to their destination. A big red truck, with four people standing in the bed, came into view. Two of the people had on helmets and chest pieces on like the riders of the motorcycles, while the other two were hooked on to the truck with harnesses.

"I see Jericho and Baylor," Mabel announced into her helmet's communications.

"How close are the other teams?" Will asked.

Mabel checked her side mirrors, "close, but I'm going to punch the nitrous."

"Have you locked on?" Kay asked.

Mabel flipped a switch on the motorcycle's steering panel, causing the bike to have two small cannons move mechanically on the seat's sides. Hooks were already loaded into the cannons, and they locked on to the armored brothers standing in the red truck. Mabel's helmet connected with the motorcycle's cannons and showed on her screen when they had finally locked on to them, with yellow squares signifying it. Before Mabel could fire, blue lights to the side of the screen started blinking.

"The Spells have locked on," Mabel didn't turn to look at the other bike.

"You need to disrupt their connection," Will commented.

"Mabel fire a hook at the bed of the truck, and reel it in. The boys should be able to jump onto your bike, and throw off the other's hooks as well," Kay suggested.

"Truck's tailgate," Mabel ordered into her helmet.

The helmet took the order and transmitted it to the bike's cannons. They relined quickly, changing the yellow square from the armored individuals, to the truck's tailgate.

"Fire," Mabel ordered again.

The cannons took the order and fired both of the hooks into the tailgate and yanked the truck back a few feet. The tires from the truck squealed with the sudden change in speed. The Spells' motorcycle fired its hooks and missed its target. The hooks smashed into the roof of the truck, scraping along the top of it. Mabel matched the speed of the truck and looked at the boys in the armor.

"Connect to them," Mabel instructed.

The helmet sent the request.

"Mabel!" Jericho screamed out, as the helmets' communications connected.

Mabel shook her head at the sudden pain in her ears, "shut up Jericho, and jump onto my bike!"

"What do you mean by that?" Jericho asked, as one of the armored boys jumped onto Mabel's motorcycle.

"Like that Jericho," Baylor said to his brother.

A hook flew between the motorcycle and truck, missing Baylor barely.

"Fine!" Jericho jumped.

Baylor grabbed his brother's arm and pulled him onto the bike. Mabel then took the opportunity to release the hooks from the truck, move away from it and avoided the other flying hooks that shot past them.

**Back to Kingfisher and Parrot Intersection – 2:43 a.m.**

Mabel rushed to pass the red truck and led the other motorcycles down the freeway while they tried to lock onto the two brothers.

"Nice steal," Will congratulated.

"Yeah, but now let's see if she can keep them," Kay pointed out.

Mabel rode around a car and steered her bike closer to the railing of the highway. She looked over the edge, as the scenery passed by in a blur.

"Tell me, Will, how close am I to Blackbird street?" Mabel asked.

The brothers followed her gaze.

"Mabel, this could be horrific," Baylor commented.

"More like crazy!" Jericho put in.

Mabel ignored them as she shifted into a different lane on the freeway, as a hook from one of the bikes soared past.

"It will be under you in five seconds," Will informed.

Mabel steered her bike right into the railing of the freeway.

"Mabel!" both brothers yelled in unison.

The bike went through the railing of the freeway, with its huge tire destroying part of it like it was nothing but building blocks. They were then free falling until the tires touched the street below them. The sudden jump made them lose some of their speed, but Mabel was vigilant enough to pick it up again. The two brothers hung on more tightly to Mabel.

"Why did you do that?!" Jericho screamed.

Mabel turned a corner sharp, and proceeded onto a new street, "because this race needs to end!"

She then turned the motorcycle onto Parrot street, and the crowd waiting at the finish line came into view. The monitors for the helmets cameras could be seen on the sidewalk.

"Wow," Baylor whispered.

Mabel rode the motorcycle through the intersection with Kingfisher street, causing the crowd to go wild with excitement and concluding the race.

"You did it, Sis," Will yelled in Mabel's ears.

"Yay, we get to keep our money!" Kay hollered.

Mabel chuckled to herself as she slowed the bike down for the first time that night. She pulled it over to the side of the street just as the crowd came upon them. The boys were pulled off the motorcycle and taken to Codie who stood in the middle of the crowd.

He took a hand from each of them and lifted them in the air, "welcome the new members of the Vital Era team!"

Cheers and whistles erupted throughout the crowd. Will and Kay worked their way through the crowd to Mabel who still sat on the motorcycle watching Codie present the brothers to the community.

"Mabel!" Will yelled.

Mabel turned her head to her brother. He could see his reflection in the black helmet.

"You okay?" he asked.

Mabel hugged Will and nodded.

# Chapter 5

**Vital Era Container August 12, 2090 – 3:52 a.m.**

The new Vital Era team entered their container full of excitement. The two brothers were still freaking out over the race, while Will listened to their enthusiasm. Kay walked over to the cot and picked up the laptop.

Mabel, Jericho, and Baylor all had removed their armor, with Baylor and Jericho's armor being returned to the council, they had on their street clothes again.

"I mean that shouldn't have been possible!" Jericho exclaimed.

"My sister is the best rider here," Will bragged.

The three boys stood at the entrance to the container. Mabel walked over to Kay and sat down next to her.

"What are you doing Kay?" Mabel asked her.

"Informing all the other teams that weren't there who won tonight," Kay typed furiously upon the keyboard.

"Really Kay?" Mabel leaned herself back against the container's wall.

"So what was that game called?" Baylor asked.

"Well, it was close to the flag game," Will said, as he sat down on the only chair in the container.

From the street, a loud bang erupted, and people laughed, but no one paid attention.

"Flag game? What does that mean?" Jericho inquired.

"Let's start from the beginning Will," Mabel instructed.

"Right, right…So the games are called Draconis. After the Draco constellation," Will started going full professor mode on the brothers, and they were absorbing it like students.

"There are three sections to the game. Race, survival, and flag. Racing is straightforward with passengers firing electromagnetic waves at other bikes to stop their engines. Survival usually doesn't involve the riders and is about who is left standing at the end of the game. And lastly the flag game. Where a package or prize is the goal, and the teams have to go and collect them before the others," Will finished explaining.

"That's intense," Baylor said.

"Do you guys play in these games?" Jericho asked.

Mabel shook her head, "we don't anymore. We just fix gear now for money."

"Take that Jeb," Kay muttered to herself as she continued to type on the laptop while ignoring the conversation around her.

"Why don't you play anymore?" Baylor asked.

Kay stopped typing, she and Will looked to Mabel. She gave them a sad smile.

"We suffered a crash last year, and we haven't played since that time," she answered.

The boys' excitement simmered down.

"Oh," Baylor looked embarrassed, "we didn't even think about stuff like that."

"Most people try not to think about it," Will mumbled, "or are trying to forget."

"Did you get hurt?" Jericho asked.

Mabel shook her head, "my bike was behind the bike that got hit. I didn't get hurt, but I was there watching the other rider bleed out."

Kay closed the laptop and stood up, "I think it's time for us to go back to school."

**Seagull Drive – 4:19 a.m.**

Mabel rode the scooter with Will and Kay holding on, while the brothers used their dirt bike. Baylor steered it, while Jericho checked his phone.

"How did you guys find us?" Will inquired, "I thought we would have lost you."

Jericho looked up from his phone, "I tracked you. Remember we exchanged numbers the first day."

Will nodded, and Kay slapped the back of his head.

"Hey, what was that for?" Will said defensively.

"You exchanged numbers with this guy?" Kay gave him an annoyed look.

Will rubbed his head, "hey, he was nice to me…It threw me for a loop."

The vehicles neared the school, and Mabel turned into Ridder Mansion with the boys close behind. The trio got off the scooter, and the brothers got off their bike.

"Well, you better take that bike back to the place where you got it from," Mabel pushed the scooter behind the wall of the mansion.

"I thought we could put it with your scooter," Baylor said.

Kay and Will gave him a strange look, and Mabel walked from behind the wall to the brothers.

"Why do you think that?" Mabel grew serious towards them.

"Aren't we part of the team now?" Jericho pointed out.

Mabel chuckled softly, "you guys are not part of this team. You simply got to have a look, and now you both will go back to the life you were living before you foolishly followed us."

The brothers' faces turned to shock.

"But what if we want to be part of your team?" Jericho stepped up to Mabel.

"That isn't your decision," Mabel didn't back down.

Baylor walked over to Kay and Will, as they watched the other two get closer together.

"We all just went through a crazy race, and now you are telling me it was all for nothing. Then why even bother doing it?" Jericho narrowed his eyes.

"We are nice people who didn't want you two to get hurt," Mabel patted Jericho's shoulder, "and we're smart, we know better than to let star students join this team because of the unwanted attention it would bring."

The two of them continued to look into each other's eyes even after they went silent.

Baylor leaned over to Will and Kay, "so you guys agree with this."

"Yup," Kay and Will said together.

Before any of them could speak again, a flashlight beam shot through one of the school's windows. All five of them hit the ground waiting for the flashlight to go out before moving again.

"Time to get back in jail," Kay whispered, as everyone stood up and ran across the street to Golden Sierra School.

**Meditation Classroom– 8:36 a.m.**

The Meditation classroom had three windows facing the west, so the morning sun didn't bother the room. It made for the perfect place to nap in the morning and Mabel, Will, and Kay knew it.

The three of them laid on yoga mats, completely asleep in the middle of the room. They were wearing their school's uniform as they laid there. The professor sat on a mat at the front of the classroom. He was in deep meditation and didn't realize that his students were sleeping. Other students in the class were doing their own thing too, and not even caring if the others slept through the period.

A knock on the classroom door didn't disrupt the teacher or class. And no one got up to answer the door. After a few seconds, the door opened, and Jericho and Baylor peeked into the classroom.

They were shocked to find the classroom in no real order. Just some kids hanging out.

"Are we sure we're in school still?" Baylor asked.

Jericho searched the room before responding, "yeah we are, there's the three of them sleeping on the mats."

The two brothers walked into the room quietly and snuck past the professor in his meditation state.

"Mabel," Baylor whispered.

"Maybe we should wake up Kay," Jericho suggested.

Baylor gave him a funny look, "you think she's going to be happy we woke her up. I think the best thing to do is wake up Mabel. She's less likely to bite our heads off."

Jericho shrugged his shoulders, "and why not Will."

Baylor shook his head, "Mabel is the one we need to convince about our membership with the team."

Baylor knelt down and tapped her shoulder. In a quick reaction, Mabel grabbed Baylor's hand and brought him down hard onto the mat.

The room became silent in the same moment, but the fellow students in the class were used to the behavior of the trio. The students went back to their conversations after seeing it was just Mabel.

"Baylor!" Mabel whispered furiously.

"Hey Mabel," Jericho smiled at his brother who was still being held down on the mat.

Mabel released Baylor, and the two of them stood up.

"You two better get back to class and let me sleep before I get my professor to throw you out," Mabel yawned.

The two brothers looked at the meditating man.

"You think you could get him to do that?" Baylor asked.

Mabel shrugged her shoulders, "why did you wake me up?"

"We wanted to convince you to let us on the team," Jericho explained.

Mabel chuckled and sat back down, "ain't going to happen."

She laid down and went back to sleep before the brothers could protest the decision. They walked away from the sleeping students.

"We need to impress her," Jericho pointed out.

"True," Baylor opened the door, "what do you want to do?"

**Principal Denzil's Office – 10:01 a.m.**

Jericho walked into the front office and up to the desk where the secretary was. He gave the older woman a charming smile.

"What's wrong now Jericho?" the secretary asked.

"Hello Mrs. Stevenson, I want to report that I saw a gun on school grounds," Jericho continued to smile, even as Mrs. Stevenson became nervous.

She got up from her desk and went to Denzil's office door and knocked.

"Come in!" Denzil yelled, and Mrs. Stevenson walked in.

The two of them weren't in there long, and they both came out quickly. Denzil was wearing her gray dress suit that went well with her dark gray spiky hair.

"Now Jericho where did you see the gun?" Denzil asked directly.

"It was in the dumpster behind the shed next to the gym," Jericho informed.

"Okay stay here, as we go to check it out," Denzil nodded her head to Jericho.

Denzil and Mrs. Stevenson rushed out of the office, leaving Jericho alone. He continued to smile as he walked past the secretary's desk and went into Denzil's office. It had dark gray walls and floor. Two hard chairs were in front of a desk that held a computer. And it had one window to add a little sunlight to the cold interior. There wasn't anything personal in the whole room.

Jericho walked over to the window in the room and opened it. Baylor climbed in next to his brother.

"So what did you put in the dumpster?" Jericho asked.

"A squirt gun," Baylor shrugged, "it was all I had."

"It should do," Jericho walked over to the computer and sat down in Denzil's seat. He started typing on the keyboard.

"Denzil left her browser open, this will be easy," Jericho smirked.

Baylor walked to the door and looked out.

"Okay, here we go, student records. Changing Business Law to meditation, and done," Jericho paused.

Baylor looked back to him, "what's wrong?"

Jericho's smirk faded, and his face became clouded with concern, "are you sure you want to trade band for meditation? You're a really good sax player."

Baylor softly chuckled, "I promise I won't miss it for one moment. Band was just a filler for me and nothing else."

Jericho nodded and went back to typing on the keyboard, "changing band to meditation."

Jericho clicked on a few more things, "and now it's done."

"Good, I think you need to get back to the front office Jericho, so they don't get too suspicious with you," Baylor walked over to the window and climbed out.

Jericho locked it behind him and walked out of Denzil's office after putting the computer back to the screen it had been on originally. He walked over to the front of the secretary's desk and waited for the principal to return.

**Art Classroom – 10:37 a.m.**

Mabel rested her head on her palm as she sat in art class behind an easel with a canvas on it waiting to be painted. The teacher at the front of the class was so focused on teaching that she didn't realize that half of her students weren't paying attention. And lucky for the brothers the door to the classroom was at the back, so the teacher didn't notice Baylor and Jericho sneak into the room and walk softly to Mabel.

Baylor tapped Mabel lightly on the shoulder, causing her to turn towards them groggily.

"Well, you two don't give up," she said sleepily.

Jericho handed her two pieces of paper. She sighed and took them from him.

"How do you guys even have this energy? You stayed up as late as me, and I'm barely making it through the day," Mabel mumbled.

Baylor and Jericho shared a look between them.

Baylor shrugged his shoulders, "the excitement we felt last night just won't go away, I guess."

Mabel gazed at the papers a few minutes before looking back up at the boys, "what am I suppose to be looking at?"

Jericho's expression changed to concern, and he tapped the paper, "our class schedules. We changed it so we could have meditation with you guys."

Mabel tilted her head, "why?"

"So we can nap when we have the long nights," Baylor explained.

Mabel sighed, "I said no."

The boys' expressions seemed to change into a puppy dog pleading expressions, and Mabel found herself falling for their faces.

Mabel shook her head, "I guess if you were willing to switch your classes, that might be in your favor for winning me over."

"So we can join?" Jericho perked up.

A student glared at them for talking, but they didn't notice him as they continued the conversation.

"Not yet, I need you two to understand that once you become part of this, it becomes your whole life.  Are you willing to do this?" Mabel asked.

"Yes," Jericho answered as Baylor nodded.

"Fine," Mabel told them, "we are going to go back out in four days, so you better be prepared to stay up all night, and be drowsy the next day, as well as keeping your grades up."

"We can do that Mabel, you don't have to worry about us," Baylor reassured her.

"Well, the two of you better get out, before the teacher realizes you're even in here," Mabel waved them away.

The brothers walked away from Mabel and quietly left the room without the teacher noticing it.  Mabel shook her head and turned her attention back to her blank canvas and sighed, as she dozed off again.

# Chapter 6

**Golden Sierra School, August 16, 2090 – 11:46 p.m.**

A security officer walked the dark halls of Golden Sierra School, with his flashlight showing him the path he was taking. He passed a door that led to the outside of the school grounds and continued down the hallway. He didn't seem to hear or notice the students following him.

Baylor, Jericho, Mabel, Will, and Kay all were watching from around a corner, as he made his way down the hall. They had been on his tail for the last twenty minutes, with a few close calls.

"He sure is slow," Kay complained.

"Shh," Mabel punched her in the arm.

The security guard walked around the opposite corner and disappeared from their sight. They ran to the door and opened it. All five of them ran out the door, only to wish they hadn't gone through it.

Two guards were walking towards them. The group was lucky they hadn't been seen, but there wasn't a lot of time.

"Go for the bushes," Jericho dove head first into nearby bushes.

The others followed him, diving in. Everyone settled to the ground, waiting to see if they would be discovered. The guards walked by them, and to the door. They opened it and went inside the school.

"Oh my, that was close," Will whispered.

"I don't remember there being that many guards the night we snuck out," Baylor mentioned.

"I believe a memo was going around campus about security, but I didn't get a good look at it," Kay informed the group.

"I wonder why?" Mabel mumbled to herself.

"Let's go, I think we can make it to the mansion," Jericho popped out of the bushes and started running along the side of the school, with the others following behind.

"Wait!" Will whispered.

Kay grabbed Jericho's shoulder quickly and pulled him against the school wall. He hit the wall a little hard, Jericho gave Kay an annoyed look. She pointed up, and the whole group looked. A camera was above them. It rotated slowly.

"Okay, go," Will said, as the camera rotated away from their path.

The group ran as fast as they could. They made it to the street quickly and didn't stop until they had made it behind the Ridder Mansion wall that their scooter and bike were behind. Everyone was breathing heavily.

"Holy Crap, that was annoying!" Kay screeched.

"We need to get going," Mabel stretched her back.

Baylor picked off leaves from his brother's clothes.

"Do we need to be this quick?" Jericho asked.

"If we want to make money tonight, we need to get there as fast as we can," Will explained.

**Cashe Corner, August 17, 2090 - 12:05 a.m.**

The scooter and dirt bike sped into the Cashe Corner section of Palaco city. Kay rode the scooter with Will and Mabel on it, while Jericho guided the dirt bike with Baylor holding on to him.

"That was close!" Will yelled.

"Yeah, has that ever happen to you guys before?" Jericho asked.

"Yeah, and we've been caught before," Mabel answered.

"Really!?" the two brothers yelled out in unison.

The trio looked at the duo, as their faces displayed their shock about the response. Will chuckled.

"There's a reason those security measures are there," Kay smirked at them.

"So you caused the school to become more self-aware?" Baylor asked.

"We were clumsy in the beginning, and let me tell you we couldn't count the number of times Denzil caught us personally," Mabel said.

Jericho made a funny face, "and she still lets you come to school after all the trouble you guys cause?"

"Well, Denzil gave us a pass," Will said.

"Why?" Baylor asked.

"Cop!" Mabel yelled.

Kay rode the scooter down the nearest alley, and the boys skidded the bike to a stop to make the same turn. They rushed down the alley, all the way to the other end before coming out one street over. Kay stopped the scooter so they could look back down the alley.

The boys brought their dirt bike up next to them and looked in the same direction.

"Why are we waiting if they're nearby?" Jericho asked.

"To see what direction they are going," Mabel informed him.

The team watched for several seconds before a cop car passed their gaze. It moved slowly in the opposite direction.

"Good," Kay mumbled, as she started driving the scooter again.

The boys followed closely behind them. They rode in silence. A sudden appearance from the cops could make anyone go silent.

"Should we be concerned?" Baylor continued to look back to see if they were being followed.

"Maybe," Will responded, "when doing something illegal, a cop always makes the situation more intense."

"Illegal?" Jericho inquired.

"You think the games we play at night are legal?" Kay chuckled, "I mean we speed and break things the city owns all the time."

"Not to mention we took over one of their junkyards," Will added, "but I don't think they care about that one."

"I guess we didn't think about that part," Baylor snickered.

"Well, you guys can't turn back now, even if you wanted to," Mabel warned them, she glared at the two brothers.

"Don't worry, we aren't thinking of leaving," Jericho said nervously.

"Good," Mabel nodded and looked back to the road.

**Vital Era Container – 12:22 a.m.**

Kay and Jericho pulled the container's doors open. They all walked into the container with Baylor, Will, and Jericho sitting on the cot, and Kay sitting on the only chair there. Mabel pulled the chest out from under the cot and opened it up. Inside were suits of armor sets for Kay, Will, and Mabel, in three compact squares with the black helmets sitting on top of each of them. There was also a lot of tools scattered about the chest.

"Those are yours?" Jericho asked as he and his brother peeked over the lid of the chest.

"Yeah, and we are going to make you both your own sets," Mabel started rummaging around the tools.

"Are you guys going to start playing again?" Baylor inquired.

"Hopefully not, but it's always good to have armor for your teammates on hand," Mabel pulled out a fabric measuring tape, "okay I need you two to come and stand in front of me."

The boys got up from the cot and stood in front of Mabel; she started taking their measurements like she was an old-fashion tailor.

"How long will it take to make the suit?" Jericho asked.

"Well, about two days or so," Mabel continued to measure them up.

Kay opened the laptop and turned it on. She started typing on it.

"What supplier should I look into?" she asked over her shoulder.

"Whoever can get the parts here tonight, I don't want to wait," Mabel took out a piece of paper from her pants' back pocket and started writing down the measurements she had just taken.

The brothers sat back down on the cot next to Will, who had been looking at his phone the entire time they had been in the container.

"It seems the Magic team lost tonight," Will announced from his phone.

Mabel and Kay each gave Will a funny look, while Baylor and Jericho remained unaware of the significance of the statement.

"That's not good," Kay mumbled.

"Why not?" Baylor looked to Mabel for the answer.

She sighed, "they are our neighbors, they rarely lose, and we just fixed some of their gear lately…Hopefully, that doesn't come back to bite us in the butt."

"I don't know Sis; the race went pretty wild. Couldn't say what happened," Will continued to look down at his phone.

"It's not like we can say that the stuff won't break. Everything breaks in this world and the armor used here isn't an exception," Kay stood up from the chair and folded her arms.

Jericho leaned over to Will, "is Kay mad?"

Will sighed, "no she just looks mad when she gets irritated."

**Petal Junkyard – 1:16 a.m.**

"Don't let that cheap win go to your head!" Kassidy yelled outside the Vital Era Container.

"That's bad news," Will said.

Mabel and Kay walked outside the container just as a can of oil flew by their head and into the Vital Era container. This caused the boys to rush to the entrance. Kassidy stood in a small group with some of her teammates, arguing with a man and a woman from the Travelers team in the middle of the road.

"Cheap win, that's bull!" the woman exclaimed.

"Our equipment was tampered with," Kassidy threw a cracked helmet on the ground.

Mabel watched it closely. It rolled into a gutter, and she walked over to it. Will joined her as she picked it up to look at it more closely. The shatterproof glass had cracked, making the screen on the inside useless, and making it impossible to communicate with the bike or other team members.

"Oh look the culprit returning to the scene of the crime!" Kassidy yelled at Mabel and Will.

The siblings looked at their accuser.

"Now that's crap!" Kay yelled, she walked right up to Kassidy and placed herself between the siblings and her.

"Oh look their watchdog has come to bark," Kassidy sneered at her.

Baylor and Jericho walked over to Kay and stood behind her, giving her their support. Mabel shook her head at the whole situation and strode over to the heated argument. She lifted the helmet up, so it caught the attention of everyone there.

"This glass is compromised," Mabel threw it to the ground. It shattered on impact. The whole group went silent.

"We don't use glass like this as a rule," Mabel continued, "Kassidy we didn't do that to your helmet."

Will strolled up to the group, and picked the shattered helmet up.

"It's not even yours," Will showed Kassidy the back of the helmet.

She looked and saw the letters 'KP' together in red.

"Wait a second," she grabbed it from Will, "my initials were in pink not red…Who did this!?"

She looked around the area until her attention went back to Mabel. Mabel shrugged her shoulders.

"I'm not sure. That glass would have been easy to get, but it would have been hard to make the helmet from it without any mechanics knowing, and all mechanics know it's against the rules to use anything else other than shatterproof glass," Mabel explained.

"So for someone to sabotage me like this, it would have taken a lot of effort just to do it?" Kassidy asked.

Mabel nodded, "Codie needs to hear about this."

"Oh don't worry, he's going to hear about it," Kassidy stormed off.

Her team and the Travelers followed closely behind, leaving the Vital Era in the street.

**Cashe Corner – 3:36 a.m.**

The scooter and dirt bike remained quiet as a cop car drove past their hiding place. Baylor and Jericho sat on the bike watching through the alley as the cop went through their view. Kay, Will, and Mabel sat on the scooter, but Mabel wasn't watching the danger that was close to them. Will notice that his sister was distracted, and he bumped her on the arm to get her attention. She looked at him and gave him a curious look.

"Okay, the cop passed," Kay said, "but we should wait a few minutes before we get back on the streets."

"Sounds good to me," Jericho stretched his back.

"Hey, how did you know that Kassidy's initials were wrong?" Baylor inquired.

"We just barely fixed her helmet, and how we keep track of the helmets is by the initials they put in them," Will explained.

"So everyone does that?" Jericho asked.

"Yeah, for the most part," Kay answered, she started her scooter's motor, signaling Baylor to start the dirt bike.

"You haven't said a word since it happened, you alright?" Baylor asked Mabel.

They made their way to the street and started driving back to school. Mabel shook her head.

"To make a helmet like that takes dedication, it couldn't have been an accident," Mabel looked down at the road, her mind taking her somewhere else.

"You sure it's not just a prank?" Jericho asked.

"One of the reasons we use shatterproof glass is because it makes it easier to form the helmet, everything else that we tried to make it with would fracture or become brittle and break," Will informed the brothers.

"So someone had to know that, to complete the helmet, right?" Baylor became more concerned with the subject.

"Yeah, and either a mechanic helped them, or they are a mechanic," Mabel went quiet.

"What I don't get is why someone would take the time to do that? It's just a waste of time and money. That loss didn't do anything to the Magic team, other than hurt their pride a little," Kay muttered.

"Disorder," Will answered Kay's question.

"Disorder?" Jericho asked.

"That's the only thing I can get from it," Will said.

"Someone was trying to cause trouble deliberately, and this isn't trouble that would just simply go away once it happened," Mabel looked up to the sky, "it was harmful trouble. Someone's not thinking right."

The group crossed an intersection and moved into East Waterside section of Palaco City. Other than the sounds from the engines of the scooter and bike, the group became silent.

# Chapter 7

"I had no idea how boring this class was," Jericho complained.

The team sat on yoga mats in the classroom. It was a typical day, other than the fact that the team hadn't gone out last night. They were finally wide awake during the class time.

"Why didn't we go out?" Baylor had a deck of cards in his hands. He was flinging the cards in the air as he laid on his mat.

"We can't go out all the time, we need to take a break from it," Will stretched his back, "we have to mix it up, so we don't get caught."

Mabel and Kay were playing hangman between their mats, on a piece of paper. Mabel was guessing while Kay held the pencil.

"You cheated, you use Jinx," Mabel tackled Kay to the ground.

The two girls started wrestling around on the floor in a playful manner as the boys watched.

"Jinx is four letters, not five," Jericho pointed out as he peered at the paper.

"Don't bother," Will sighed, "Kay didn't even write down a word. She just put spaces."

"How can you tell?" Jericho pulled the paper close to him.

"All the vowels were guessed, and none of them were used. It couldn't be a word," Will sighed again at his sister and friend.

"So, why even play the game then?" Jericho gave the entangled girls a strange look.

"They're bored too," Will shrugged his shoulders.

The two girls separated from each other as Mabel's phone rang. Mabel took it from her bag and opened the phone.

"A text from who?" Will peeked over Mabel's shoulder.

"It's from the Draconis council," Mabel whispered.

"Oh, what's wrong?" Kay looked over Mabel's other shoulder.

Baylor sat up, while the brothers waited for the news.

"We have been requested to play in the games tonight," Mabel read the text, "we will be in a survival game."

"That's not good," Will whispered.

"Well, we're screwed," Kay stood up from the mats and straighten her burgundy hair.

"Why?" the two brothers asked.

"We need to get one of their suits of armor ready now," Mabel stood and picked her bag up.

"The helmets are ready, and the major pieces of the suit just need to be wired, if we work on it now it will be ready," Will explained.

"We just skip next period and get it done before the night even comes," Mabel said, as she walked out of the classroom.

Jericho leaned over to Baylor and asked, "should we follow them."

"Really May, that's going to be a lot of work in a short amount of time," Kay followed Mabel out with Will right behind her.

"I'm thinking yes," Baylor said to his brother.

**School Shed – 9:14 a.m.**

The shed, the team had taken over, was behind the school and looked completely out of place because its exterior was old and rustic.  It didn't go well with the sleek outside of the other school buildings, but that was what made it a great place to work.  No one noticed it, and that was why the Vital Era team was inside working loudly without a care in the world. The inside was dusty and smelly, but the teenagers didn't seem to mind.

They had placed several tables in the shed; tools and pieces of a silver armor were on tables. Mabel held a helmet while sitting on one of the chairs in the room. Kay and Will were at a different table trying to fix a short circuit inside a chest piece of armor.

Jericho watched Kay and Will working on the chest piece. Baylor sat on a chair next to Mabel, watching her fingers work carefully with the screws being put into place.

"You know there's two of us," Jericho said.

His eyes went over the armor, as Kay and Will looked up at him. They each gave him a confused look.

"And here I thought there were three of them," Kay sarcastically said.

"That's not what I meant," Jericho punched her lightly in the arm, "I only see one set of armor here. Are you guys just making one?"

"Yes," Will answered quickly, "and the reason is that right now we only need to create one. For tonight, the game won't require all of us, and this is all we can get done at the moment."

Jericho nodded in agreement, "so you are going to make a second armor? Just later?"

"Yup, we have the material for it, the wiring just takes up a lot of time. So we are getting done what we can," Kay punched him lightly back.

"Will you two stop flirting," Mabel mumbled as she connected delicate wires in the helmet before setting it down.

Kay gave Mabel a death glare, as Jericho's face turned red.

"Oh my goodness," Will gasped as he ducked away from Kay's punch.

Baylor picked up the helmet, "can I put this on?"

He asked the question to stop Kay from hitting Will or Mabel. Jericho thanked his brother silently for changing the subject.

"Really?" Mabel asked.

"Well we are skipping second period, I think a reward is needed," Baylor handed it to Mabel.

Mabel smiled at him, and took it from his hands, "stay sitting."

Baylor didn't move from his seat as Mabel held the helmet above his head. She brought it down slowly and softly, as the other three watched closely, placing it on the top of his head she continued to push until it slid all the way down.

"How does it feel?" Mabel asked.

Baylor moved his head around, "great, that's a great fit."

He held a thumbs up.

"Good," Mabel said.

"This feels heavy for a helmet," Baylor pointed out.

"That's good," Mabel responded, "this armor will be heavy, it's designed to keep you alive if you crash."

"That sounds like a bulletproof vest," Jericho said.

"I think it could stop bullets if needed," Will suggested.

**Vital Era Container, August 23, 2090 – 12:28 a.m.**

Will, Kay, Jericho, and Baylor stood in the container in full armor, except for their helmets. The silver exterior shimmered in the lights from outside. All of their armors glowed yellow and had yellow ribbons wrapped around their waist. Mabel sat on the chair in the container; she was connecting one of Jericho's gloves, so it joined the power going through the suit, while Baylor looked himself over in awe. Kay walked over to the table; it had two pairs of bracelets and a pair of ankle bracelets on it.

Kay took one of the bracelets and clicked it on to her wrist. She pushed a few buttons, causing brown lights to come on signifying the device's power. Kay placed the other bracelet on her other wrist, and its brown light came on when connected. She took the ankle bracelets and started putting them on.

"What are those?" Jericho asked.

"Well," Kay began.

"Before you get technical Kay," Mabel interrupted, "let's tell them about the positions, then gear."

Kay sighed dramatically, "fine. There are four positions in the games as a whole. A rider, a heavy, a foot, and a eagle. And there are also four different categories someone can be in. Now the gear is related to the categories."

Will picked up the other set of bracelets on the table and started putting them on. The bracelets' lights glowed red instead of brown.

"The categories are knight, soldier, wizard, and the newest one, kinesis," Kay continued. "Now with the different positions and categories, there is different gear, except for the riders because everyone uses the bikes. Knights have a bow for eagle, a knife for foot, and sword for heavy. Wizards have potions for eagle, wand for foot, and staff for heavy. Soldiers have a rifle for eagle, knuckles for foot and baton for heavy. And lastly, Kinesis has fire for eagle, water for foot, and earth for heavy."

"That's a lot to take in," Jericho commented.

"So in other words, the eagle is long ranged," Baylor asked Mabel to see if he was getting it right, "the foot is up close, and the heavy can deal great damage?"

"Yup, you got it," Mabel smiled at him, "okay Kay now you can tell them about us."

Kay sighed dramatically again, "our team is Kinesis, and we are the only one in the category. Now I'm a heavy. So I use rock gear to play."

Kay stomped her foot hard on the ground; the ankle bracelet released brown light that formed a rock next to her. It stayed steady, almost looking like it could be touched. She then clutched her fist and moved her arms in a sweeping motion towards the back of the container. The brown light rock moved in that direction in a quick motion. It disappeared when it smashed into the wall.

"Holy crap!" Jericho and Baylor exclaimed.

"Now you show them," Mabel said to Will.

Will replaced Kay in her position in the container, "I'm a eagle, so I use fire."

He brought his fist together in front of himself, and his bracelets released red light that surrounded his wrist and moved like fire. He then punched the air in front of himself sending the red light fire to the back of the wall where it disappeared.

"That's insane," Jericho couldn't believe what he was seeing.

Mabel laughed a little, "well now it's your turn to gear up."

**Skate Park – 1:52 a.m.**

Will, Kay, Jericho, and Baylor walked into a temporary stadium. It covered the entire skate park. It was like a colosseum with metal bleachers in a circle. A huge crowd sat in the bleachers screaming and yelling. Two other teams were already getting in position, with wooden platforms placed all around the park. The Secret team glowing purple with purple ribbons, and the Ravens glowing blue with blue ribbons.

"We got the Secret team which is a knight class, and Ravens team which is a wizard class," Will's voice said through the communications in the helmet of all his teammates.

"Good to know," Kay moved behind a wooden platform. Jericho and Baylor followed, while Will climbed to the top of one and looked out at the area.

"Okay guys, don't worry about winning this," Will said to the brothers, "we won't lose anything if we don't win."

Jericho had gear like Kay, and he was getting himself ready, "no worries, we got this."

Bing! A loud sound came from the bleachers, signaling for the fight to begin.

Will turned his bracelets on and started firing his light at the other opponents. Flashes of light started going across the field. Kay powered her gear up, stepped out from behind the platform and ran across the skate park. Jericho looked out from behind his platform.

He saw two blue armored people with small cauldrons strapped to their waist. Their hands would go in and pull out white light that looked like a bottle filled with blue dust. They would aim the bottle then throw, and it would fly through the air at its target unaffected by gravity. They were firing at Kay who was pinned down behind a platform. Baylor saw it and stepped out from his hiding place. His gear was different from the others. It looked like he had two water pouches strapped to his sides that were made out of metal.

He had techno gloves on that glowed blue, and he brought them to the pouches opening. In a swift motion, he pulled out blue light from one of the pouches, that looked like water, as he ran up to the two blue armored people. Baylor jumped onto the platform with them and hit both of them with the same blue water light. The light disappeared on contact, causing the blue in the suits to turn off. The two people were powerless and out of the game. They jumped down from the platform and started making their way to the exit. Baylor jumped down.

"Good job, Baylor," Kay said.

An opponent with purple armor charged at Jericho, as they held a metal handle in their hand with small light coming from it. The handle had a purple beam of light in the shape of a sword at the end of it. Baylor ran to his brother and pushed him out of the way as the sword was stabbed in his chest. The sword's light returned after the opponent pulled it away. Baylor's suit went dark.

"You're out of the game Baylor," Will informed him, "you need to exit the park."

**Sidelines at Skate Park – 2:18 a.m.**

Mabel watched Baylor's suit go dark, and run out of the park. Mabel stood on the metal bleachers surrounding the entire skate park. The metal structure wasn't the most secure, as it wobbled and creaked with the constant movement from the crowd, but no one noticed because of the excitement on the playing field.

Jericho and Kay moved to a different platform as two purple armored people charged them. They both held knife hilts with short glowing purple blades. Will released his red light fire at them, protecting Jericho and Kay.

"It looks like your team is doing good?" Joi commented.

Mabel jumped a little at seeing her suddenly in a purple dress and black leggings.

"You scared me; I haven't seen you around lately," Mabel observed.

"And I thought you stop playing," Joi turned her attention back to the game as did Mabel.

Will managed to hit one of the knife wielders, as a huge spell attack smashed into his armor and powered him down. A blue armored individual stood on a platform carrying a metal staff with a sphere at the top glowing the same color as the armor. Will jumped down from a platform and ran to the exit.

"Tough loss," Joi watched intensely.

A purple armored individual holding a bow jumped onto a platform and pulled the string back, causing a purple arrow of light to appear. It was released and sailed towards the staff wielder. The arrow missed, but the bow was quickly reloaded. The second arrow hit its mark, causing the staff wielder to go dark on the field.

Kay and Jericho started throwing brown light rocks at the bow wielder. They missed as the two of them took cover. When suddenly the sword wielder came charging at them. They both dodged the first attack, and before the sword wielder could try again, a blue light smashed into the sword wielder causing their armor to go dark. A blue armored person stood on the nearest platform with a wand pointed at them.

Kay and Jericho both threw rocks at the blue armored individual, with one of the rocks hitting them in the chest and powering down the last blue suit on the playing field.

"The Ravens are out," Joi mumbled, "good for you guys."

"We still have the Secret team," Mabel pointed out.

And as if on cue, a sword wielder and knife wielder ambushed Kay and Jericho. Both were powered down before anyone could react. The crowd went wild as the game came to an end.

But during the chaos, Mabel noticed Joi remaining calm. It unsettled her, as Joi's reaction to the game was abnormal.

Mabel touched her shoulder to get her attention, "you okay?!"

Joi smiled at Mabel, "Fine!"

Joi and Mabel exited the bleachers and stood outside of the park so they could hear each other.

"Mabel," Joi started, "you should stop playing the games."

"Why?" Mabel's face showed her surprise.

"It's going to be bad for your health," Joi smiled sadly, "I got to go."

Mabel watched her walk away in confusion.

# Chapter 8

Mabel walked around the perimeter of the skate park until she came into view of the entrance to the playing field. The teams, who had been on the field, were now standing around talking to each other about the game with their helmets off. The Ravens, standing in their blue suits, congratulated the Secret team, with their suits glowing purple.

"You know you had a great game today," a Raven teammate said.

"Thanks, you guys were hard to beat though," a Secret teammate returned the compliment.

Mabel walked around them and to the other side of the small group of armored people. She came into view of her team. They were sitting down on old box containers trying to catch their breath. Baylor and Jericho were both sweating greatly, while Will and Kay were just a little hot.

Mabel came up to them, "you guys did great!"

"Thanks, we didn't do too bad," Kay stretched.

Before anyone could say anything else, a loud alarm went off. It sounded like the alarm that signified a tornado approaching, but this one had a different meaning.

"What's that?" Jericho asked.

Everyone who was in the bleachers started scrambling to get off them, and people ran onto the field, going to the wooden platforms and breaking them down. As soon as everyone was off the bleachers, the metal beams were collapsed, and the whole structure was separated into three sections, which were each compacted down until they could be carried away.

"We need to get to the container now!" Mabel ordered.

"Why?" Baylor asked he became part of a crowd running for the junkyard a few blocks away.

"The police are coming!" Will yelled in his ear.

The crowd surged away from the skate park like it was on fire and there was no water to put it out. Panic was pulsing throughout the crowd, causing some people to scream out but everyone pushed forward. Nothing could stop their stampede. Kay held onto Jericho's hand, as she pushed through the crowd, and Mabel held Will's hand while he held Baylor's arm.

The team was making their way down the street. The orange light from the streetlights casted an eerie glow upon them. With all the bodies so close together it looked like a mad mob of brain-eating zombies trying to catch their prey.

"We're almost there!" Mabel shouted over her shoulder, "hang on; we need to make it to our container before they cover everything up."

"Cover up!?" Baylor's suit protected him from the bumps he was getting from the crowd.

"It's the safety protocol," Will yelled to him.

**Vital Era container – 2:54 a.m.**

Mabel pulled Will and Baylor into the Vital Era Container, with Kay and Jericho right behind them.

"Power down now!" Mabel ordered, she walked back out of the container.

"Wait, where are you going?!" Baylor tried to grabbed Mabel's arm.

But she slammed the container shut on him. The team was now in the dark with their glowing yellow suits the only light. Mabel placed the latch over the container's doors but didn't lock them. She went over to the rope ladder that connected the two containers above and climbed up it.

Mabel made it to the top where Kassidy, in her yellow tank top and sweatpants, was laying on the container with Brenton next to her, who wore an orange sweater and pants.

"Hey May," Brenton greeted, as Mabel laid down next to him.

"Are you ready for this?" Kassidy asked she looked nervously at the street.

"No," Mabel answered, "but we need to do it anyway. Are we waiting for the other containers to get ready?"

Kassidy nodded, "but we are going in five minutes either way. We have to make sure this works before it gets too late to do anything at all."

The three of them watched as people scrambled for safety, and as the leaders of teams closed the doors on their group and made their ways to the tops of the containers. Everyone seemed to be nervous as everything was being shut, and lights were being turned off. The street went dark, but no one screamed at the sudden change.

"I guess now is the best time to do it," Kassidy said to the other two.

The three of them stood up and went over to the wall of garbage that surrounded the junkyard's perimeter. They each took a rope that connected to planks of wood holding the wall in place. Sounds of crashing garbage could be heard from other places on the street.

"I guess it's started," Brenton pointed out, "let's do this, one, two, three!"

The three of them pulled on the ropes, which pulled the planks of wood from the wall. In seconds the wall of garbage tumbled over on top of them and covered the containers. Mabel pulled herself to the top of the garbage and looked it over in the moonlight. Everything looked covered, all she could see now was a sea of trash.

"Covered!" she hollered down the street, before going back into the garbage.

She wiggled herself back to where Kassidy and Brenton were in the pile. They could just barely see the street.

"Does it look good?" Kassidy asked.

"Yeah, we are in the clear," Mabel informed them.

**Petal Junkyard – 3:07 a.m.**

The whole junkyard was dark. And the wall that once surrounded the area was gone, but the street in the middle of the yard was still intact.

The area looked like it had suffered an avalanche with the garbage standing tall and covering every container.

Leaders from all the teams were hiding in the trash, waiting for any signs of trouble. This was the safety protocol that their community had put into place. And for the last few months, it hadn't been needed or tested. Making the situation even more stressful.

Mabel could still feel the metal container under her, but her eyesight couldn't see anything through the trash or darkness. But a flash of light caught her attention. From where she was in the pile, Mabel could see two officers walking slowly down the dirt road in the middle of the junkyard. A man in blue overalls walked with them, he was part of the community and had been assigned to be the owner of the place, his name was Jeb.

A beam of light from one of the officer's flashlights went around the huge piles of trash. It felt like a searchlight at a prison. They neared the spot where Mabel hid with Kassidy and Brenton. Mabel looked down on them like a vulture waiting for their prey to die.

"You know officer, I did hear some loud noises, but they were everywhere. I couldn't pinpoint what direction," Jeb lied to the officers.

"Thank you, sir for your input, but we still need to check the area out," one of the officers explained.

"Yeah we had an anonymous tip come in that this area was crawling with the biker gang that has been tearing up this city," the other officer added, "so we had to come."

Mabel's heart went to her ears, as she became more nervous at hearing the officers talk.

"Well, I don't know what to tell you," Jeb went along, "all that's here is junk. There aren't any motorcycles here. Trust me, I would know. I'm a motorcycle junky myself."

"Yeah, what's your favorite?" the officer asked, as the three of them continued to walk down the road.

Their voices no longer reached Mabel's ears, but she was still on high alert. These officers had been the closest the police had ever been to Mabel and her team. It was a rule around the community that you avoided cops, for if the cops got suspicious of you, it could mean your career was over in the games.

"Mabel?" Brenton whispered in her ear.

"What?" Mabel whispered back.

"Do you think someone in the neighborhood snitched on us?" Brenton kept his voice low and close to her.

"Don't know," Mabel turned her attention back to the police officers coming back down the road.

**Seagull and Albatross Intersection – 4:23 a.m.**

"Clear!" a loud voice yelled.

Mabel, Kassidy, and Brenton jumped out of the trash and maneuvered to the top container in their section. Other leaders from different teams were doing the same thing in their areas. Mabel and Brenton dug around where the doors should be, while Kassidy pushed the garbage away. In a matter of minutes, they had the top container's doors uncovered. Kassidy opened up the container. Inside were her teammates, they all scrambled out.

Kassidy then locked the doors and continued to help dig out the other containers. Brenton's container was next, and they were able to open it up and let everyone out.

"Okay, one last one," Kassidy announced, both the Soldiers team and Magic team were helping dig now.

The trash was cleared, and Mabel pulled the doors open. Will, Jericho, Kay, and Baylor all stood there in their street clothes. They had changed from their suits of armor.

"Let's get going," Mabel ordered.

At that small command, the other two teams that had been helping clear the trash hurried out of the junkyard. Mabel walked to the side of the containers and pulled out the red scooter. A little bit of trash came with it.

"What happen?" Jericho asked Kay and Will worked the dirt bike out.

Baylor helped dust off the scooter.

"Two cops entered the junkyard," Mabel answered, "we need to get out of here as fast as we can."

Kay closed the doors to their container and locked it up with a padlock. Jericho got on the dirt bike and started it up, while Mabel got on the scooter. Will and Kay jumped onto the scooter, while Baylor got onto the bike.

"What about the containers?" Baylor looked back at them.

Jericho and Mabel rode their vehicles down the dirt road.

"Someone from the junkyard is going to come and cover all the containers back up," Will explained.

The small group rode out of the junkyard with several other teams scurrying away as well. They made their way down one of the streets.

"Did anyone say how the cops got called?" Kay asked Mabel.

Mabel nodded, "I heard one of the cops say they got a tip saying that our community was in the area. But I don't know how they knew to check the junkyard. That part doesn't make sense."

"Would someone have heard us in the junkyard?" Jericho inquired.

"We aren't next to any apartments or housing development. The junkyard is in an industrial area. People aren't here during the middle of the night. No one would even be walking their dog here," Will explained the concern.

Mabel sighed, "let's just focus on getting back to school in time."

**History Classroom – 8:09 a.m.**

Mabel, Kay, Will, Baylor, and Jericho ran down Golden Sierra School's hallway. They had showered so the trash smell wouldn't be on them and had on their school's uniforms on. The bell for the first period had already rung, meaning if they were found they would be marked late.

"We'll meet up at lunch," Mabel said, as they passed several classroom doors.

"Yeah, just don't fall asleep," Kay stopped at a classroom door and peeked in before opening it and quietly sneaking in.

The others kept running down the hall.

"I don't think I will be able to sleep tonight at all, with the adrenaline from last night," Baylor commented, as Will and he stopped at a different door and went quietly into a room.

"See you at lunch," Jericho stopped and rushed through a classroom door.

Mabel turned a corner and stopped at the first door. She looked in through a tiny window. Her history teacher was teaching at the front of the class, his ruler in hand, pointing to a black and white photo of the Civil War.

The door was at the back of the classroom, so Mabel waited for an opportunity to sneak in when the professor was looking at the board instead of the class. He turned his back, and Mabel opened the door quietly.

"Now see, the reason there were so many photos taken during this time was the camera had recently been introduced to society," the teacher stated.

Mabel passed several other students until she got to her empty seat. She seated herself softly and placed her bag on the ground next to her. She quickly pulled out a pen and paper. Her professor stopped looking at the board and turned back to the class.

"But because of the time it would take for a photo…" he paused in his lecture, "oh I see that Ms. Overton has decided to join us."

"Hello Professor Fletcher, I'm sorry for my lateness, but I had to visit the nurse's office for some health problems this morning," Mabel gave him one of her best smiles.

Fletcher shook his head, "this happens so often Overton. I am beginning to think that you have mixed up your classroom with the nurse's office."

Mabel chuckled a little, "Professor Fletcher you are quite humorous."

The students in the room remained silent, as they watched Mabel and Professor Fletcher talk.

"I'm writing you up, Overton I am tired of your lateness and won't tolerate it anymore," Fletcher walked over to his desk and started writing something down with a pen.

Mabel sighed. She put her paper and pen away and stood up from the desk. Picked up her bag and walked to the front of the room. Fletcher handed her a slip of paper.

"Detention!" he thundered.

# Chapter 9

"I mean seriously, we were only late by a few minutes, and it was only our third time. I don't get why they had to give us detention," Kay complained.

The small group of Will, Mabel, Jericho, Baylor, and Kay sat on benches in the school's garden area. Bushes and flowers surrounded them, giving the area a sweet smell to the air. They were sitting on two benches on the sides of the path. Will, Baylor, and Jericho shared a bench, while the girls shared the other.

"I heard they were going to get strict with tardiness, so I guess that means less flexibility with how many times someone can be late," Jericho pointed out.

The group had on their school's dark blue uniforms, while they sweated in the sunshine of the day. They each had lunch trays on their laps, as they tried to eat mashed potatoes and mystery meat.

"I wonder why they've focused on that rule?" Baylor stood up and walked over to a trashcan; he dumped his tray into the bin.

"Well, we might have caused the crackdown because of last year," Will said to Baylor, "we caused a lot of tardiness for some students."

"Why did you do that?" Jericho asked.

"So we wouldn't look suspicious, but don't worry we stopped doing it," Kay explained.

Baylor sat back down next to Will, "what would you do?"

"Oh, lock the bathrooms so no one could get ready. Jam a door or two. You know stuff that couldn't be linked back to us," Kay shrugged her shoulders.

Mabel, who had remained silent during the conversation, finally looked up at her team. They seemed fine after the incident at the skate park, but the team hadn't gone back since the police.

"I have news about the games," Mabel announced to the group.

The conversation going on between them stopped, as they turned their attention to Mabel.

"There's going to be a flag game tonight, and we have been asked to participate in it," Mabel looked around the group, "I haven't said anything back to them."

"Why?" Baylor asked.

"With what happened, I believe it should be our team's decision if we go back. It's been several days since the police, but I didn't know how you guys felt?" Mabel answered.

Jericho sighed, "Maybe we should skip tonight's games?"

"And I think we should go," Kay stood up, "it was only two officers. That isn't anything to worry about."

"I'm with Jericho," Will said.

"Seriously!" Kay yelled.

"Well I'm with Kay," Baylor said to the group.

"Ha!" Kay pointed at Jericho, "now we're tied."

Jericho smirked at Kay before turning his head to Mabel, the rest of the group looked at her too.

Mabel shook her head, "I do believe, we should be fine if we go out tonight, but I also think we need to be cautious. Those two cops weren't nothing."

Jericho nodded, "fine. I will concede."

Kay smirked at him, "and what about you Will."

"I don't like it," Will stated, "but we could use the money if we win."

**Crane Alley – 10:52 p.m.**

A cop car drove slowly down the street as if they were waiting for something to pop out in the night. The orange streetlights made that thought seem believable, on the quiet streets.

The Vital Era team was waiting for the cop car to pass. They hid in an alley, behind two dumpsters. Jericho and Baylor were on their dirt bike, while Kay, Will, and Mabel were on their scooter. They could just barely hear the cop car going down the street. It didn't stop, but everyone became a little nervous.

The cop car made it to the end of the street and turned a corner; giving them a little relief.

"So should we go?" Kay asked Mabel.

Mabel shook her head, "let's stay for a few more seconds."

"Do you want to turn around?" Will looked at his sister.

"We can," Baylor chimed in, "no harm done."

"I think we still should be fine," Mabel answered, "it's just one cop, that isn't anything new or unusual."

"True, besides I've wanted to see others from the games," Kay said.

"Won't we need to clean up the garbage?" Jericho asked.

"We can go now," Mabel told Kay and Jericho.

They both started up their engines and rode out of the alleyway. They rode under the orange lights, casting strange shadows that followed them.

"We don't need to clean up the garbage; someone else would have done that," Will called over to Jericho.

"Yeah, the wall of garbage has to be put back in a certain way, so someone who knows how to build the wall cleans up the junkyard. No worries about that for us," Kay continued Will's explanation.

"That's good to know," Baylor said.

The team turned a corner and neared an intersection where a lot of activity was taking place. It was part of the games; people were setting up monitors for the future audience to see the action. The Vital Era team stopped by the sidewalk to talk to the people.

"Hey Vital Era, I didn't think we would see you here," Debbie called out.

She stood up from wiring the monitors and walked over to them. Her hair was still orange-red and spiky.

"We decided to join tonight's games," Mabel said to her.

"Cool, well three of you better get suited up then. One rider and two passengers tonight for the flag game," Debbie waved goodbye as she went back to working on the monitors.

"Who's playing tonight on our team?" Jericho inquired as the group started driving again.

"Well Mabel for sure, and I'm going to be playing as well because I'm an eagle," Will said, "but I don't think you or Kay will be playing because your equipment so that only leaves Baylor."

"Really?" Baylor asked in shock.

"Yeah, that sounds right," Mabel smiled.

**Mockingbird and Parrot Intersection – 11:56 p.m.**

The sides of the street were filled with people cheering and yelling. There were monitors at the corner on the sidewalk, but everyone was paying attention to the street. Four of the modified motorcycles were there. Each bike had three people on them in full suits of armor.

Mabel, Will, and Baylor sat on their motorcycle in the middle of the group. They were doing last minute checks before the race started. Mabel sat in the front, and Baylor sat between the two siblings on the bike.

"So who we racing tonight?" Baylor asked through the helmet's communication.

"We have the Seal team in green at the end, the Horsemen in blue next to them," Will answered, "and the Camo team in brown on our other side. The Seal and Camo team are soldiers while the Horsemen are knights."

Mabel revved the motorcycle's engine; it caused a cheer to rise from the crowd. Mabel smiled to herself.

"I haven't seen Kay or Jericho yet," Will looked through the crowd.

"Get ready Will," Mabel said.

The three of them turned their attention to the crosswalk, as a man walked to the center. He held up a long white rag. It moved a little in the wind.

"Get ready!" he yelled, "get set! Go!"

The bikes didn't stay another second, all four of them sped down the street. It seemed like even the light was trying to keep up with them. Will powered his bracelets, as a member of the Camo team powered up a rifle next to them.

Mabel maneuvered around a parked car and rode on to the sidewalk. She avoided benches and other items, as Will fired his light fire at the team. They returned with brown light bullets from their gun.

"I don't see the other teams anywhere?" Baylor watched Will and the other player exchange attacks.

"They probably are off attacking each other on a different street," Mabel said, she forced the motorcycle off the sidewalk and pushed ahead of the Camo team.

"Why did they do that?" Baylor ducked as a light bullet went over their heads, "I thought this was a race."

"It is, but it's a race that doesn't have a destination yet," Mabel turned a corner sharply, "we are still waiting for beacons to be dropped."

The two motorcycles continued down the street. They both were neck-in-neck. But Mabel changed the bike's speed, so they slowed suddenly, giving Will the opportunity to hit the other bike with his light. His light fire hit the rifle wielder, causing their suit to go dark. Will then hit the other teammates holding on, causing their suits to lose all power.

"Good job Will, that's one team out," Mabel congratulated.

**Freeway, August 31, 2090 – 12:28 a.m.**

Mabel went across several streets and rode the motorcycle through the city. Two green lights blinked onto her helmet's screen; they indicated where they needed to go.

"Okay, I got the two beacons, get ready for the real battle to begin," Mabel announced to the other two.

"Which one are you going for?" Will asked.

"The ten thousand one," Mabel turned a corner sharply again and entered the freeway.

"Do they always put the beacons on the freeway?" Baylor asked.

"No," Mabel answered.

Beeping in Mabel's helmet alerted her to the other two motorcycles coming up, "Will get ready."

Will looked at the other two and started firing at them, the two bikes both fired attacks. Mabel weaved between cars on the freeway.

"It seems everyone is going for the ten thousand tonight," Mabel commented.

"Yeah, I guess whoever is left, will just get the five thousand," Will said.

Just as Mabel passed an SUV, a red truck came into view.

"Okay, Baylor you are going to jump onto that truck, and grab the tube that is strapped to the roof," Mabel informed Baylor.

"Oh," Baylor hesitantly said, "okay."

Mabel rode right up to the truck as flashes of light sailed pass them. But Baylor didn't notice them, as he jumped onto the truck in a quick motion. He steadied himself, before gripping the tube strapped to the roof of the truck. He started working on pulling it off.

But his efforts were interrupted when two grappling hooks from one of the bikes smashed into the bed of the truck and jerked it around. Baylor lost his grip and fell back into the bed.

"You okay?" Mabel asked.

"Yeah," Baylor said over their communications.

The jerking of the truck continued, and the grappling hooks tried to pull it closer. Baylor stood up, hanging on to the sides, and pulled himself back to the roof. He unclipped the tube from the truck's roof.

"Incoming!" Will yelled over their communications.

All three of them ducked, as a flash of blue light went over their heads. The Horsemen motorcycle sped up next to them, as Will started firing back at them. A bow wielder was firing at them. Baylor watched them for a second, before grabbing the edge of the truck.

"Don't jump yet!" Mabel ordered him, "I'm not close enough!"

"Just catch it!" Baylor tossed the tube to Mabel.

"Baylor!" she screamed as she maneuvered the motorcycle to catch it. They ended up farther away from him.

But before they could get back to him, a blue arrow shot across the freeway and hit him in the chest. Baylor's suit went dark as he lost power.

**Cashe Corner – 12:41 a.m.**

Mabel didn't wait another second after Baylor's suit lost power. She sped away from the truck. The Seals' bike left them alone as they slowed down to try and get the other beacon, but the Horsemen's bike didn't give up the chase. It charged towards them, as both teams weaved between cars.

Mabel passed the tube to Will, who grabbed it. She revved the motorcycle's engine before moving closer to the side of the road. The Horsemen remained on their tail. Grappling hooks flew from the

Horsemen's motorcycle but missed their mark. The sound of them being reloaded clicked behind Mabel and Will.

"We need to get off the freeway," Will commented.

"An exit is coming up!" Mabel moved the bike to dodge a light arrow.

The Horsemen drew closer to them, but Mabel braked suddenly. The other motorcycle shot forward with their grappling hooks being shot into empty space, Mabel accelerated to the freeway exit causing the Horsemen to miss the exit. They started making their way back to Cashe Corner.

"Now we just need to get back to the intersection," Mabel said.

"That was a good move," Will looked back at the freeway as they sped away, "where did you learn that?"

Mabel turned a corner, "when you and Dad were on that fishing trip, I practiced my driving technique."

"Thank goodness," Will smirked.

Mabel rode onward, coming to an intersection with a red light. They didn't stop at the light but passed through the intersection without any hesitation. Yellow light from their bike seemed to trail behind them as they moved through the streets.

"We are coming up to the finish line," Mabel announced to Will.

"Do you think Baylor will be fine?" Will asked.

"Yeah, the truck will bring him back, heck they might get there sooner than you think," Mabel reassured.

Turning one last corner, Mabel and Will came into view of the intersection they had started from. The crowd was still on the sides cheering as they rode into the area and stopped. They were instantly surrounded by screaming people.

Kay and Jericho worked their way through the crowd until they were standing next to the motorcycle. Mabel and Will unclicked their helmets and pulled them off.

"Good job!" Jericho yelled.

"We're rich!" Kay screamed.

Mabel chuckled at Kay and Jericho's different reactions to the race's results. The energy coming from everyone was very intoxicating, making the past troubles seem like nothing to them.

# Chapter 10

**Mockingbird and Parrot Intersection August 31, 2090 – 12:57 a.m.**

The crowd still surrounded Mabel, and Will as the red truck with Baylor on it drove into the intersection. Baylor jumped out of the bed and worked his way through the crowd to his teammates. He joined in the celebration with them. The excitement was overwhelming.

A woman got out of the truck and climbed onto the bed so she could see above the crowd.

"Shut up!" she yelled.

Her yell was taken up by several others until everyone settled down enough for her to be heard.

"It's time to award the prizes, so Vital Era come up and Seals," she waved them towards the truck.

"Kay, go for us," Mabel stepped off the motorcycle.

"No problem," Kay walked up to the truck with swagger.

She jumped onto the bed and stood tall as the crowd cheered. A member of the Seals team climbed onto the truck as well.

"First place goes to Vital Era," the woman handed Kay a black bag, "and second place goes to Seals."

The Seals teammate was handed a black bag too, the crowd went back to yelling and hollering, as the woman got off of the truck. Kay and the Seals teammate jumped off of the truck too.

"Cheaters!" came a scream from within the crowd.

That single yell made the crowd go silent without any help. A man, from the Camo team, came forward in a suit of armor with no power. He had a woman and a man behind him in powerless suits as well. They walked up to Vital Era team and glared at them.

The man pointed a finger in Mabel's face, "you guys cheated, and you know it. You're nothing but frauds!"

"That's quite an attitude you have," Mabel said calmly, "maybe you should watch the recording before you get so heated."

The man tried to reach for the bag Kay carried as she came back to the group, but she kept it from his grasp.

"Don't you dare," Kay warned.

"That should be ours," the man said angrily, "cheaters like you don't deserve it and you know it."

Mabel and Jericho placed themselves in-between Kay and the man.

"We earned that bag Andrew," Mabel's face became serious, "we don't take things that aren't ours."

"Why you," the man, Andrew, raised his hand.

But before he could bring it down, it was caught by a different man.

"Winfred!?" Mabel looked at the newcomer in surprise.

Winfred looked at both sides before speaking, "if there is a problem here, we take it to Codie for a ruling."

"Fine, let's go to Codie," Andrew growled.

**Draconis Container – 1:32 a.m.**

Mabel and Andrew stood in the dimly lit container. Mabel's silver suit glowed yellow, and Andrew's suit remained dark. Codie sat behind the desk with his old leather jacket on, watching the recordings of tonight's game. He watched it on his phone quietly and with a solemn face, while Mabel and Andrew waited for his conclusion on it.

After sighing, Codie turned off his phone and placed it on the desk. Looking up, he gave them both a curious look.

"So, Andrew why do you think Vital Era cheated?" Codie asked.

"Because, during the race, just before the beacons were dropped, they did a move that was out of line," Andrew complained.

"And what move was that?" Codie continued to question.

"When she braked her bike and went behind my team. Giving us a complete disadvantage," Andrew pointed out.

Codie sighed again, "and when has that move ever been called illegal in the games?"

Andrew stopped talking as shock started to fill him. Codie turned his attention to Mabel as he let Andrew recover from the shock.

"Mabella, what do you have to say about this?" Codie inquired.

Mabel shook her head, "that move has happen before with no complaints. I don't understand why now it's a problem. If Andrew thinks it should be illegal, then maybe that should be looked into. But if this is because he's a sore loser, then let it be."

Andrew gave Mabel an angered look, "a sore loser. You dimwit! What you did was wrong, I'm trying to make it right!"

"Dimwit! Like you would know any better numskull!" Mabel yelled at him.

"You pig-headed…" Andrew yelled.

"Silence!" Codie ordered.

The two of them stopped their insults. Codie stood up from his desk.

"From what I have seen in the footage, and with our laws here. I have to side with Vital Era," Codie announced.

Andrew through his hands in the air, "of course you side with Mabella. You have always been sweet on her because of how she helped you build these games!"

"That's not it!" Codie shook his head, "if you think a move like that should be illegal in the games take it up with the council. But right now after a loss, there are no grounds for it."

"Bull crap!" Andrew stormed out of the container.

Mabel watched him leave without saying a word.

"This is going to be bad," Codie mumbled, he sat back down in the chair.

Mabel looked back at him, "I don't understand. I mean their team has never caused trouble like this before. But now all of a sudden they're sore losers."

Codie sighed once more, "something is in the air. You need to watch out Mabella."

Mabel chuckled to herself, "you know. You aren't the first person to say that to me."

**Vital Era Container – 1:46 a.m.**

Mabel left Codie's container. She walked down the dirt road, deep in thought. People along the roadsides stared and whispered among themselves. After several yards, Mabel started to notice the whispering.

She looked at the individuals who whispered and watched them as they wouldn't meet her eyes. It became obvious to her that word had spread about the ruling on the game. The sudden attention unnerved her, and she started walking faster down the road.

Mabel reached her container and rushed in. Kay, Jericho, Will, and Baylor all stood in the container. Baylor and Will had changed out of the suits of armor and stood in their street clothes like the others.

"Do we get to keep the money?" Kay asked she held the black bag close.

"Yeah we do," Mabel looked back at the street, and saw a small group of girls staring.

They moved away when Mabel made eye contact with them. Mabel shook her head and sat down in a chair. Will went over and started disconnecting her armor. The rest of them sat on the cot and started going through the bag.

"What did Andrew say?" Will asked.

"That we did an illegal move," Mabel answered she pulled off her arm armor.

Will worked her leg armor off and placed it on the table, before working on her chest piece. Mabel unhooked her waist section of armor and placed it next to the other pieces. She was finally free.

"Well at lease Codie sided with us," Kay gleefully said.

A couple of men walked slowly in front of the container. They looked in with judgment in their eyes. Mabel saw them, as did Will.

"What is with everyone?" Will asked.

"I don't know, but maybe we should think of leaving," Mabel stood up and straightened her street clothes.

Jericho gave Mabel a funny look, "we don't usually leave by now. What's wrong?"

Mabel shook her head again, "Andrew was mad at the ruling, and I think he might be spreading rumors around."

"Really?" Baylor tilted his head, "I thought this community was above gossip."

"No community is above gossip," Kay sighed.

She stood up and opened up the trunk under the cot. Placing the bag of money in it and Mabel's armor, she locked it up with a combination lock.

"Okay, let's get going," Kay waved them all to leave the container.

Everyone got up and moved out. Kay and Will closed the doors and Baylor placed the padlock on the latch.

Jericho walked around to the side of the container, and pushed out the scooter, while Mabel pushed the dirt bike to the road.

**Glass Bridge – 3:46 a.m.**

Mabel sat up from her bed and looked around in the dark. They had made it back to school, with enough time to sleep before classes started. The boys had gone back to their rooms, and the girls had gone to theirs.

Kay slept soundly in her bed, but Mabel hadn't been so lucky she had continued to toss and turn as the night continued to move on without her. Sleep was avoiding her.

Mabel pushed back her blankets and stood up. She pulled on her shoes and walked out of the room. The hallway was dark, but she was still able to find her way through. There wasn't a specific destination in mind; her body just wanted to wander as she remained restless. The hallways on the second levels didn't have as much security as the first floor, so nothing hindered Mabel's wandering, as she walked onto the second floor.

Something felt off to Mabel. The night had started fine, and nothing in the race had seemed wrong. But a team coming out and calling them cheaters hadn't happen before. Vital Era's reputation had always been good, with very few complaints. And now someone had called them cheaters, and the Magic team had accused them of making faulty parts.

Something was going on in the community, and the Vital Era team was receiving a bad reputation for it.

Mabel walked past several classroom doors until she came to the glass bridge that was in the middle of the campus. The glass shimmered in the night with the light from the city. She walked to the middle of the bridge and sat down on the floor.

The dark sky and lights from the city calmed Mabel's mind. It was just a small relief from her troubles. Time passed slowly, and the view changed at a gradual pace. Streaks from the sunrise filled the sky, causing some of the city's lights to turn off.

Mabel sighed and stood back up. She dusted off her pajama pants and started walking back to the girls' dorm. The problems hadn't gone away, but the relief had been worthwhile. The hallways were still dark as she made it back to her room, and Kay was still sound asleep as she reentered.

She went back to her bed and pulled the blankets over herself. Mabel released a quiet sigh. Something was off, and it was bigger than minor problems like one game or one helmet. And it was building up to something more radical.

Mabel closed her eyes and tried to sleep.

**Lunchroom – 11:45 a.m.**

The lunchroom was full of students waiting in line or eating at the tables. Noises from the room could mask the sound of gunshots if they were to happen. Mabel quietly sat as she waited for the others to come to the table. She had managed to go through the line for food before them. Will and Baylor came walking up an aisle between the tables. They were talking. The two of them sat down with Mabel between them. Their conversation continued, but Mabel didn't listen. She was still waiting for the others to come.

Kay and Jericho walked down a different aisle, before sitting down on the other side of the table. The two of them looked happy, with smiles on their faces.

Mabel looked around at the group and felt bad that she would soon take their excitement away.

"We need to talk," she said to the group.

Her simple words stopped all conversation, as her teammates focused on what she was going to say.

"What's wrong?" Will's face became covered with concern.

Mabel shook her head, "we are going to stay away from the games for a while."

The excitement of the group went down as Mabel's words affected them all differently.

Kay began to fill with anger, "why?! Just because someone called us a cheater!"

Kay stood up from her seat, "I mean seriously, what does it matter what they think anyway?"

Mabel gave Kay a distressed look, "it's not about what they think. I don't feel good about going there. We need to take a break from the community."

"That's a bunch of crap!" Kay turned away from the table and walked away.

The group watched her go in silence. Will looked at his sister.

"Do we have to stop?" Will inquired.

Mabel nodded. Will lowered his gaze, and got up from the table. He left the group and the lunchroom.

"Will we ever go back?" Jericho asked.

Mabel cringed a little at the question, "I don't know."

Jericho left the table after her response. Baylor watched him go and sighed. Mabel started to tear up, and she wiped her eyes.

"So, now what do you think you'll do?" Baylor asked.

Mabel shrugged her shoulders, "I don't know. Something is wrong. I can feel it."

"Fine," Baylor nodded, "then we should wait."

Mabel sighed and stood up from the table, "I need to have a moment to myself."

She left Baylor alone. He looked down at his hands, before standing up from the table and following his teammates out of the lunchroom.

# Chapter 11

Kay, in her street clothes, dusted off the scooter, so the red paint shined in the orange light of the street. A week of dust had covered it, and Kay wanted to make sure none of it was on the scooter. She worked on it with a rag. Jericho stood in his street clothes too, as he watched Kay clean.

"We should have taken better care of them," Kay mumbled to herself.

Will pulled the dirt bike from under the blanket and pushed it to the driveway of the mansion. He wiped the dust off with his hand and onto his pants, before sitting on the bike. The engine came to life, as he started it up.

"You should clean it, we don't want the other teams to think we're sloppy," Kay warned.

Will rolled his eyes. Baylor straightened his shirt before looking at the bike's gas gauge.

"I think it's fine for tonight," Baylor looked up from the gauge.

His eyes went to Mabel as she stood on the sidewalk looking at the school. She didn't stare at it for danger. Something still felt off to her about the games.

"Okay," she said to Baylor.

Kay gave Mabel a glare, before finishing the scooter's cleaning, "the scooter's fine too. Not that you care."

Mabel didn't seem to hear Kay's insult, which caused Kay's mood to get worse. Jericho and Will exchanged a concerned look between themselves as the mood changed. Kay got onto the scooter and started the engine too. It came to life, but not as dramatic as the bike.

"Jericho, Baylor, you're riding with me," Kay ordered.

The two brothers gave each other helpless looks before getting on the scooter. Kay didn't wait for another second after they were on, she rode down the mansion's driveway and passed Mabel. She didn't look at her team captain as the scooter went down the street.

Will sighed at Kay's attitude. He pushed the dirt bike until it was next to Mabel.

"You ready?" he inquired.

Mabel finally turned her head and looked at Will. Her face was full of concern. She shook her head but got on the bike anyway. Mabel took the main seat.

"Hey, if you don't want to go, you don't have to. We aren't planning on doing any games tonight, so you could stay behind," Will suggested.

"Will, get on the bike!" Mabel ordered.

They were her only words that night with any emotion, and they had sounded harsh to Will. He got on the bike and held onto his sister, but now his feelings of going to the games had been tainted.

**Petal Junkyard – 11:43 p.m.**

Mabel stopped the bike. They had made it to the entrance of Petal Junkyard. Will got off the bike, and she followed after him. The two of them started walking down the dirt road in the middle the junkyard. It was busy like usual with people everywhere. The containers all looked to be open, and there didn't seem to be anything negative around. But Mabel remained in her mood.

"I wonder where the others are?" Will gave his sister a funny look.

Mabel didn't respond to him. She just continued to push the bike.

"Why do you have to be moody?" he mumbled to himself.

"You aren't listening to me," she finally answered.

Will became a little taken aback, "we listen to you."

Mabel shook her head, "Will, let's not talk about it. There's no point, we're here now and must deal with the consequences of that."

"When have you been afraid of consequences, May. I mean building this entire community was a hazard, but now all of sudden you don't like taking chances?" Will couldn't believe his sister.

"That's because it's changing," Mabel stopped pushing the bike so she could look at her brother, "something isn't right. And it's not just us who are getting the worst of it. Those cops coming a few weeks ago weren't of the blue and shouldn't be taken so lightly."

"You're overreacting!" Will stormed down the road, away from Mabel.

She watched him leave before shaking her head. Pushing the bike along, Mabel let out a sigh. The night had started off hard, and it appeared it was going to stay that way.

"Hey Mabel," a young man's voice called.

Mabel continued to push as the young man came up to walk beside her. He looked like a normal guy from off the street, for his hair was naturally black instead of a bright color.

"What's up Louis?" she asked him.

"I was wondering if you could take a look at my gear, it's been acting weird for the last few days," he explained.

"We aren't taking orders right now," Mabel answered, "go to the Blacksmiths their good with gear."

"I already did, they have a huge waiting list," Louis complained.

"Well then, I guess you're going to have to wait, Louis. I'm sorry, but we aren't working tonight. If we come back tomorrow we can look at it then," Mabel said.

Louis gave her a dissatisfied look, "fine. I'll go to someone else."

He walked away from Mabel. She didn't stop or sigh. It wasn't the time for business, and she knew better than to look at a suit of armor. The team would be working on it for the rest of the night, and they were all in a bad mood already.

**Skate Park September 13, 2090, – 1:56 a.m.**

Mabel sat down on the rattling metal bleachers next to Baylor. Jericho, Kay, and Will were on the other side of him and did not acknowledge Mabel. All five of them were sitting instead of standing up, like everyone else in the crowd around them. They weren't paying attention to the game going on.

"Hey May," Baylor greeted.

Before she could respond, everything changed. Spotlights turned on and blinded everyone in the crowd. Police officers flooded the playing field, and several rushed onto the bleachers.

"Everyone's hands up now!" a voice yelled over a speaker system.

The crowd of people erupted. Everyone scrambled to get away from the army of officers, causing the entire area to go into chaos. People jumped off the bleachers and onto the playing field, others tried to exit them, but the cops were bringing down anyone that got close to them. The people in power suits started firing their weapons at the officers, with officers returning fire from their weapons.

The Vital Era team stood up and started working their way through the crowd to the other side of the bleachers, and away from the cops. But their progress was stopped, when the entire metal structure they stood on collapsed. The beams broke, and everything fell into a heap, including the people on it. Screams and yells gave way from the pile of debris.

Mabel pulled herself out from underneath the rubble with her brother on her back.

"Will, you okay?" she asked him.

Will limply held on to her back, "yeah, I think I'm fine."

Mabel worked her way out of the pile of rubble before looking back. People were running all around her, and the screams from the area were increasing, but her attention was only on the pile. She looked for any of her other team members, while others worked their way out of the mangled mess.

Baylor stood up from the wreckage holding his arm.

"Baylor!" Mabel called to him.

He saw her and made his way to her. She grabbed his hurt arm and started pulling him away from the skate park.

"What about Jericho, and Kay?" he puffed out.

Mabel directed them through the chaotic crowd. Avoiding officers and panicking people.

"We can't wait," she said to him.

They left the rubble, just as Kay pushed several metal pieces off of her. Blood dripped down her forehead, and she was being supported by Jericho. His face had scratches on it. They worked together to get out of the metal. The two of them then started going in the opposite direction of the others.

**Cashe Corner – 2:22 a.m.**

Will still limply hung onto his sister's back, as she and Baylor hid behind a dumpster in an alley.

"Help!" someone screamed as two officers pushed a man to the pavement.

Mabel watched as handcuffs were placed on him.

"What should we do?" Baylor asked, his breathing was still heavy.

"We need to focus on getting to our meet up point," Mabel whispered to him, she ducked behind the dumpster again.

"I didn't know we had one of those," Baylor sat down.

"Yeah, we forgot to tell you two," Mabel sat down next to him.

Will groaned a little as Mabel shifted him to a more comfortable place as he stayed on her back. He didn't have any blood on him, but there was a bruise forming on his forehead.

The officers in the street stood the man up and walked out of sight. Mabel and Baylor waited five minutes before moving from the dumpster. They walked slowly to the edge of the alley and looked down the street. Officers turned the corner away from them, looking for others trying to escape.

"Okay, come on," Mabel walked in the other direction at a brisk pace.

Baylor walked behind her, while still holding his injured arm. Keeping low, they made their way through Cashe Corner. Sounds from the chaos echoed down streets and alleys, giving the buildings an eerie feeling. The buildings gave off the feeling that they watching the streets, and it affected everyone running around including Vital Era.

Mabel turned a corner quickly, before disappearing into an alley. Baylor struggled to keep up, as she went to an intersection of alleyways.

"Where is the meeting point?" Baylor leaned against a wall while Mabel listened to the sounds going on.

Sirens from cop cars passed by and more yelling seemed to come from everywhere.

"It's just across that street," Mabel pointed to a street that a cop car rushed down, she hung onto Will with her other hand as he unconsciously laid on her back.

The two of them walked to the edge of the alley and cautiously looked both ways on the street. It was empty, and they took that opportunity to cross it, rushing over, they made it to the other side.

"Did you see anyone?" Mabel removed Will and placed him against a wall.

"It was all clear," Baylor leaned against a dumpster.

Mabel went over to the dumpster and knelt down beside it. She pulled out a crowbar from underneath it. Taking it in hand, she placed herself above a manhole cover. Placing the crowbar at the edge, Mabel lifted the cover up, so the sewer was exposed.

"Get down there," she ordered Baylor.

He nodded and climbed down, using the metal ladder already there. Mabel put the crowbar back under the dumpster and went to her brother. She picked him up and walked back to the sewer. She handed him down to

Baylor, before starting down herself.  She pulled the manhole cover back over, so no one would know anyone was in the alley.

**Parrot Alley – 2:31 a.m.**

Kay sat behind garbage cans, while Jericho rested on the other side of the alley behind a dumpster.  They both were breathing heavily as they waited for the cops on the street to move on.  But the officers had formed a group right next to the alley's entrance.  Kay and Jericho couldn't hear what they were saying, but they could hear that the officers were whispering.

"So, do you think you will need to say sorry to Mabel," Jericho whispered to Kay.

She stopped looking down the alley and sat back against the wall, "why?"

Jericho smirked as he felt the scratches on his face, "we might be going to jail.  Some people would reflect on how they manage to get themselves in such a position."

"We aren't going to prison," Kay smirked back.

"Yeah?" Jericho gave Kay an annoyed look, "well we don't even know if they have gotten caught.  But of course, it's their fault and not yours."

Kay couldn't believe Jericho's attitude, "what's wrong with you?"

Lights from flashlights danced down the alley, causing the two of them to duck down. But the lights weren't searching, as they didn't stay long and left the alley.

"My problem is the fact I don't know where Baylor is," Jericho glared at her, "and I don't know if he is hurt. But you don't seem to care if your teammates are even alive."

"That's not true," Kay shook her head.

"Really?" Jericho sarcastically said, "because your actions say differently."

The whispering of the cops faded away, and the lights from their vehicles disappeared from view. Kay stood up from her hiding place, and Jericho did the same.

"I may have actions that speak differently," Kay walked to the alley's entrance and looked both ways on the empty street, "but understand we have been through worse than this. And this is no end."

Kay met Jericho's eyes, and the two stared at each other for several seconds.

"We need to go over one alley," Kay broke eye contact and walked down the street a little.

"Fine," Jericho said in an annoyed voice.

Jericho followed Kay to a different alley, where she went to a dumpster and pulled out the crowbar underneath it. Within seconds she had the manhole cover next to the dumpster open. The two of them looked down into it.

The orange light from the street illuminated the hole. Mabel and Baylor looked up from the bottom, with Will on Mabel's back.

"You go down first," Kay ordered Jericho, "I need to pull the cover over us."

Jericho didn't say a word to her, as he jumped down into the sewer. Kay gave him an annoyed look before following behind him while pulling the manhole cover over their heads.

# Chapter 12

The East Waterside section of Palaco City was better maintained than Cashe Corner. Buildings were new, and roads were well-built. This was one reason Golden Sierra School was built in this section of the city instead of any other. But this did give the team Vital Era, a harder time to get back.

Kay, Jericho, Baylor, and Mabel walked along the sidewalks in the area. With each of them keeping a lookout for anyone that might cause them trouble. The sounds of sirens and screams had finally faded away, but their effects still made the team nervous. Mabel led their little group, with Baylor and Jericho right behind her and Kay bringing up the rear. Their small group remained quiet after reuniting.

Will was now conscious, but was being carried by Jericho. Mabel didn't want him to walk until he could see the school's nurse. The bruise on his face looked bad.

Baylor rubbed his arm and asked, "what about our container?"

Mabel didn't turn around to answer him, "I locked it before I went to the skate park."

"And the scooter and bike?" Jericho asked.

"I have the keys," Kay answered, "no one will steal them."

Jericho gave Kay an annoyed look, and she gave him one right back. The two of them were still on each other's bad side. The group went silent again. Daylight was sneaking up on the night, and soon the city would awaken.

The team didn't want to be outside, but in their beds when the city woke up. But at the pace they were going, it seemed daylight was going to win. And some of their hope had been lost with that fact.

Will rested his head on Jericho's shoulder, "do you think anyone was arrested?"

The question drifted around them, almost taking on an evil spirit.

"I know some people got arrested Will," Mabel quietly answered.

Will teared up, and started crying on Jericho's shoulder. Baylor looked at him in surprise with the reaction.

"Hey man, don't worry they shouldn't stay in jail for too long," Baylor tried to comfort.

Will shook his head, "that's not it."

Tears continued to fall from his eyes, "they will be banned from the games now. They won't be allowed into our community. Everything they worked for is gone."

Will continued to cry as Baylor and Jericho soaked in the news.

"Is that true?" Jericho looked at Mabel.

"Yes," Mabel still didn't turn around but continued to lead them back to school, "they are on the cops radar now, and the community can't have that."

Baylor and Jericho shared a look.

"There's a lot you guys didn't tell us," Baylor mumbled.

**Ridder Mansion – 7:45 a.m.**

The first bell of the school day rang, and students in the Golden Sierra School rushed to their classes. With how a tardy was being treated, no one wanted to be late.

Kay watched from across the road as everyone scurried. She shook her head and walked back up Ridder Mansion's driveway, and back to her team. Mabel was looking at Baylor's arm, while Jericho and Will sat against the wall that surrounded the perimeter.

"I don't think it's dislocated or broken, but you might have landed on it when the bleachers collapsed. Probably going to need some muscle relax lotion, and an ice pack," Mabel finished her examination.

"Okay, so where do I get those?" Baylor gave her a funny look, "you wouldn't happen to have them, would you?"

Mabel smirked a little before shaking her head, "no we don't have those here."

She walked over to Will and looked at his bruise. It covered half of his face in blues and purples. Mabel examined the wound and looked into his eyes.

"Well, I think it's just a bruise Will, I don't think you have anything to worry about," Mabel stood up and brushed her clothes off.

"What are we going to do?" Jericho inquired.

"Well," Mabel shrugged her shoulders, "I think you three are going to go to the nurse's office, after you get your school uniform on, and explain to her that the three of you fell downstairs on the west side of the boy's dorm."

"Why the west side?" Jericho gave a smirk at Mabel.

And Mabel returned it right back, "there aren't any cameras on that side."

Baylor waved his good hand in the air, "how in the heck do you even know that?"

Will answered him, "we hacked into the school's security system the first year we started sneaking out. We know where all the cameras are and when new ones are installed."

Jericho and Baylor stared at Will. Both of their mouths hung open.

"Are you serious?" Baylor couldn't believe them, "you could go to jail for that."

"With what we do, we could go to jail for a lot of things," Kay mumbled, she cleaned the cut on her forehead with the dust rag.

The two brothers looked to Kay, as shock continued to fill them. Mabel gave Kay a serious look, but she wouldn't look at any of them.

Mabel took command, "okay, you three go to your dorms and get in your uniforms. You use the path that we use to get out at night, then go down the west stairway, and straight to the nurse's office."

"What about you guys?" Jericho asked he picked himself up off the ground.

Mabel looked at Kay, "we are going to get our uniforms on and then suffer whatever consequence we get for being late."

Kay finally made eye contact with Mabel, before turning around and heading to the school.

**Girls' Dorm – 8:33 a.m.**

Mabel looked in the mirror in the room she shared with Kay and combed her hair. Kay stood at her closet straightening her collared shirt. The two of them hadn't talked since the separation of the group.

With her hair combed out, Mabel placed the brush down and went over to her bed. She picked up her jacket from the covers and pulled it on.

"If your head's hurting, you should go to the nurse," Mabel suggested, she looked at her roommate.

Kay continued to mess with her shirt and only nodded at Mabel's suggestion.

"Kay," Mabel faced her, "you need to talk to me. We need to talk about last night."

Kay stopped messing with her shirt and looked to Mabel, "I'm sorry."

The two words came out weak, but their meaning remained strong. Mabel walked over to Kay and embraced her, as the two friends hugged, Kay cried quietly. She sobbed into Mabel's shoulder.

"That has never happened before," Kay cried.

"Yeah," Mabel agreed, "that was something truly horrifying."

The two girls released their embrace and sat on one of the beds.

"Do you think people died?" Kay quietly asked.

Mabel took a few seconds before responding, "maybe. I don't know for sure Kay, but a lot happened. And we even saw our fair share of injuries."

"What does it even mean?" Kay asked.

Mabel shook her head, "I don't know. But it isn't bad luck; I can tell you that."

"What do you mean?" Kay gave Mabel a weird look.

Mabel stood up and paced the room, "someone might look at what has happened these last few weeks as bad luck, but that just can't be. The type of things that are happening isn't just circumstances. Someone is going around and causing them. But to go so far as to cause a raid on us. Is something I can't understand."

"Do you think someone from around the area has been watching us?" Kay suggested.

Mabel shook her head again, "no. No one from the outside could have done what happened tonight and the nights before. Someone has gone rogue in our community."

Shock filled Kay, "that can't be."

"There is no other way for everything else to be explained. The bad helmet, the bad race, and the cops coming to Petal Junkyard themselves. Only someone who knows our community could cause trouble that way," Mabel explained.

Kay stood up from the bed, "but who would even do this. Everyone who is a part of it is dedicated to our society."

Mabel shrugged her shoulders again, "the best I can tell you Kay, is that's not true anymore. Someone has either lost faith in us or lost faith in the games."

**Art Classroom – 9:53 a.m.**

Canvases and paints were everywhere in the classroom, and the teacher was having a hard time keeping the students under control.

Everyone in the room was covered in paint making it look like a paint fight had happened.

Mabel looked at her canvas with no emotion towards it. There were streaks of paint on it, but there was nothing special about the streaks of paint. Her teacher yelled at two students that had ruined each other's paintings. The two of them were at each other's throat for the sabotage. Mabel looked at them and shook her head.

"Idiots," she mumbled to herself.

"Hey Mabel," a female student came up to Mabel, "did you hear about last night?"

Mabel gave her a smirk, "no what?"

"Last night there was a huge bust, the police raided the motorcycle gang that has been terrorizing our city," the student smiled at Mabel, "isn't that great!"

"Terrorizing?" Mabel questioned her words.

"Yeah, they've been tearing up the city for years now. I mean all the damage they have done is ridiculous," the student couldn't believe Mabel's reaction.

"I didn't think they had done that much," Mabel looked down at her hands to hide the tears forming in her eyes.

"Oh yeah, they tore up Midtown. I mean several stoplights were destroyed, and people's businesses were broken into," the student waved a hand in the air to add drama to her words.

"That wasn't all them," Mabel looked furiously at the student.

She was taken a little aback by Mabel's behavior, "actually it was. My boyfriend is part time for the police force, and he was telling me all about how the gang smashed all the windows in the Compass Eye Shopping Center."

"That's not true," a different student chimed in, he moved his seat closer to them.

"What, you don't believe me about the motorcycle gang?" the first student challenged.

"Oh not that," he said, "that you have a boyfriend in the police force."

"You little…" she tackled him to the floor, and the two of them started wrestling around on the ground.

The teacher came over quickly and separated the two of them, "get a hold of yourselves. This is no time to fight, but to paint!"

"Teacher," Mabel said.

"Yes Miss Overton?" the teacher asked.

"May I go to the restroom? I'm not feeling the best, and I think I need a break from the paint fumes," Mabel inquired.

"Sure honey, you go ahead," the teacher nodded.

Mabel gave a half smile before leaving the classroom. She walked briskly down the hall, as tears started falling from her eyes.

"We aren't criminals," she mumbled to herself.

**Glass Bridge – 10:11 a.m.**

Mabel walked onto the glass bridge and stopped in the middle of it. Sunlight danced across the city, making it sparkle like stolen treasure. She wiped tears from her eyes as she looked out.

"Mabella?" came a man's voice.

Mabel turned sharply and saw at the end of the bridge, Codie. He looked like he hadn't slept at all, and that he had been in a fight. His face had black smudges on it, and his leather jacket was ripped on the sleeve. He walked up to Mabel.

"Codie," Mabel cried.

The two of them embraced each other.

"Is your team okay?" he asked, as they stopped hugging.

"Yeah, nothing serious," Mabel answered, "and what of Draconis games?"

Codie let out a sigh, "I don't know.  Felix died last night."

"What!?" shock completely covered Mabel's face, "how are the Vikings taking it?"

Codie shook his head, "not well.  They are blaming the police for his death."

Mabel took a moment to think, "he didn't get shot?  Then what happen to him?  He was one of the most careful leaders in the games."

"It wasn't from the police, he was fleeing with his teammates, and he ran into a street without looking and got hit by a vehicle," Codie explained.

Mabel covered her mouth with a hand, "oh my, that's terrible. Did he suffer?"

"No, he died instantly," Codie turned to look out at the city, "even when we aren't driving, we still die in the streets."

"Codie this isn't your fault," Mabel placed a hand on his shoulder, "what happened was unexpected."

Codie turned to her, "was it?"

The two of them stayed silent as the question sunk in. They had both thought similar thoughts; was someone out to destroy their community?

"I need to go, but I thought I would make sure your team had made it through the night," Codie gave Mabel another hug.

"Be safe," she whispered to him.

"You too," he released her and started walking away.

But before he left the bridge completely, a voice stopped him.

"Who are you?" Denzil asked from the other side.

The two of them turned to face Denzil. She stood in her gray dress suit, with her hands on her waist.

"Well, I came to see Mabella," Codie slowly responded.

"Really?" Denzil walked onto the bridge and placed herself between Mabel and him, "why have you come on to school grounds without any acknowledgment with the front office?"

Mabel thought quickly, "I'm sorry Principal Denzil. He was here to give me a message from my father. My old car broke down and had to be sold. That's why he looks like a mess."

Denzil turned to Mabel and gave her a questioning look, her eyes full of disbelief.

"Well," Codie scratched his head, "I need to get back to work."

Denzil turned her attention back to him, "next time you come onto school property, you check in with the front office Mr.?"

"Doyle," Codie lied, "good day."

He walked briskly away from the two women. Denzil looked back to Mabel and gave her a suspicious look.

"Mabella, I need to talk to you," Denzil started.

Mabel shook her head, "I'm sorry Principal Denzil, but I need to get back to my class."

"Fine," Denzil conceded, "get to class."

Mabel turned away and walked quickly down the hallway.

# Chapter 13

**Meditation Classroom, September 16, 2090 – 8:23 a.m.**

It was a quiet day in the meditation classroom. The professor sat at the front of the room in his meditation state like normal, and the students quietly talked among themselves. The Vital Era team was acting no different from the other students. Will read a book, Baylor and Kay worked on homework, Jericho played with his phone, and Mabel laid on a yoga mat.

It had been several days since the raid on their community, and they had somewhat recovered from it. All of their injuries were healing, with Will's bruise still slightly showing on his face. They had all calmed down. There was only one death in the community that they had heard of, and the news of no more casualties had settled them.

"So I carry this over and then add forty-two to the total, right?" Baylor asked Kay.

She looked up from his paper and glanced at him, "yeah, you got it. Man, Baylor, you're really good at math."

"Thanks," Baylor smiled.

"He's always been good at math, it's one of his strongest abilities," Jericho mumbled without looking up from his phone.

Kay gave Jericho a dirty look before going back to her homework. The two of them had been on each other's nerves, and time only seemed to make it worse.

Mabel's phone beeped from inside her bag, and all the team members stopped what they were doing. Will placed his book on the floor, Kay and Baylor looked up from their homework, and Jericho put his phone away. Mabel sat up from her mat and grabbed her bag. She searched in it for a few seconds before finding her phone. Taking it out, she read out loud the text message sent to her.

"Warehouse 62, meeting there at 1:20 a.m. tonight," Mabel read.

Mabel put her phone back into her bag and looked at her teammates. They all returned the stare.

"So?" Jericho asked, "are we going?"

No one responded as they waited for Mabel to talk. She looked around at them before speaking.

"I think we should go. We need to know first-hand what is going on in our community," Mabel paused, "and what losses were suffered."

"Okay," Kay said, "but how do we get there?  Our bike and scooter are still at the junkyard."

"What?  You guys don't have a contingency plan for this problem?" Baylor asked.

"Well," Will started, "in the early stages of our community, people would come and pick us up.  Then once we got our motorcycle working and put together, we started using that.  But that became a problem, because of how loud it was.  That was why Kay found the scooter."

Baylor and Jericho both gave Will a funny look at his long explanation on the matter.

**Bald Eagle Drive, September 17, 2090 – 12:55 a.m.**

The Vital Era team stepped out of the taxi, while Mabel paid the man who had driven them.  Kay, Jericho and Will stared up at the warehouse they were going to enter.  The night air had cooled from the day, and a sliver of moon shined down on the little group.

Mabel finished paying the taxi driver and watched him drive away with Baylor.

"Do you think he will report us?" Baylor whispered to Mabel.

"I don't think so," Mabel shook her head, "and even if he did, we were blocks away from the school. So he will have to guess what school to report us to."

They both shrugged their shoulders at each other before staring up at the warehouse like the rest of their team. The warehouse didn't look different from any of the other buildings in the area. It was huge with a flat black roof, and dark gray walls with windows on the sides every few yards.

"I don't remember the last time we were here," Kay said.

"You guys have been here before?" Jericho asked.

"Yeah, it's where we use to meet before moving to Petal Junkyard," Will chimed in, "it was a very cramped place to have all those containers. We barely fit in there, and eventually had to go four high with the containers instead of the three high we use now."

"Wow, four high," Baylor commented.

"What do you think is going to happen May?" Kay looked at Mabel, causing everyone to look to her.

Mabel sighed, "I don't know what to expect in there to be frankly honest. A lot has happened, and I know that several teams are no longer part of our community because they got arrested. But we have always been united, so hopefully, we will all make it through this."

"And what if they aren't united this time?" Baylor asked.

"If that is the case, it would be complete chaos," Mabel shook her head again, "I don't even know what we would do, and I can't even begin to comprehend what would happen to the community. The best I can guess is that what we have built, what we have worked for, would be shattered and lost."

Silence followed after Mabel's comment, and the group suddenly didn't want to enter the warehouse. The changes it held inside might be too much.

"We can't fight this off," Kay mumbled, "we should go in and hope for the best."

Kay walked up to the warehouse and opened the door. She walked in without any second thought to what could be inside or what could happen. The team members looked at each other before following slowly.

**Warehouse 62 – 1:16 a.m.**

The building was full of people yelling. Codie stood in the middle of the room, on a big box so he could be seen above the crowd. He was trying to calm the crowd down, but his efforts were useless against the waves of anger. The Vital Era team tried to work their way to him, but moving through the crowd was nearly impossible.

Joi, in her purple silk dress, climbed atop the box with Codie and fired a starter pistol. The sharp crack of the gun made the room go silent. She nodded her head at Codie and got off the box. He gave her a weird look before turning to the hostile audience around him.

"Thank you for all making the trip out here!" he yelled to the crowd, "I know all of you came to hear about the teams."

Codie took out his phone and started reading, "the teams that are no longer part of our community: Pegasus, Blacksmiths, and Ravens. Now teams who lost members: Magic, Seals, and Vikings."

The announcement astonished the crowd. Everyone received news they hadn't heard before, and everyone was trying to process it.

Will turned to Mabel, "I didn't hear about the Magic, I wonder how Kassidy is doing?"

Mabel nodded, "I hope they are okay."

Will and Mabel's conversation ended with someone yelling in the crowd.

"So what are we going to do about it?" a woman yelled.

Codie looked towards the woman, "what do you mean by that?"

She worked her way through the crowd until she stood on top of the box with Codie. The woman's name was Lacy, she was the leader of the Seals team.

"I mean what are we going to do about our losses? We can't roll over and die!" she yelled out.

The crowd cheered at her comment, with just a few teams not joining in. Vital Era and the few other teams remained quiet.

"We need to push back on those who have hurt us," Lacy ended her last two words with great emphasis, causing the crowd to start to riot.

Many were yelling to take action, making the whole crowd start to rile up. Codie watched his people start to boil.

He shook his head, "silence!"

His loud yell went over the crowd and quieted them down. Anger was in his eyes, and everyone took his sudden attitude change seriously.

"I want all the leaders to go to the back room now!" Codie ordered, "the rest of you will be calm and quiet until we come out."

The crowd did as he said, and all the leaders of the teams worked their way through the crowd towards the backroom. Mabel left her team behind.

**Backroom – 1:21 a.m.**

The backroom felt so small as the leaders of the teams entered it. There was nothing in it, and the lights flickered. Thirteen people stood in the room. They all formed a circle and waited for Codie to take charge. He shook his head and stood in the middle of the circle. Codie looked tired, and his jacket was still ripped.

"We need to talk about this calmly," he looked around, "now let's talk about the losses. Jim, how is your team holding up?"

The new leader of the Viking team stepped forward. His young face was serious and looked like it had seen a gruesome battle.

"My team is suffering," he looked around the circle, "and we want to know what will be done for our team?"

"And what do you want to happen?" Emily, the leader of the Travelers, asked.

"We want revenge," he stated.

Mabel became uneasy with Jim's statement.

"From who?" Kassidy asked, "the police? They were doing their job."

Jim rushed up to Kassidy and grabbed her by the shirt, "Felix is dead!"

"And that was by a car, not the police!" she broke his grip on her.

Codie went over and pushed the two of them apart, "both of you calm down. Jim, we understand why you feel the way you do. But we don't attack people. What do you expect us to do?"

Jim couldn't believe Codie's response, "we have suffered so much because of the police, and the laws we have to live by because of them. Why aren't you even mad Kassidy, or are you glad Garnett is no longer on your team?"

Kassidy pushed Codie out of the way and punched Jim in the face. He took the hit then tackled Kassidy in her mid-section. He pushed her towards the wall and slammed her into it. Kassidy took the impact and slid to the ground clutching her sides.

"Stop!" Codie grabbed Jim by the collar and threw him to the circle's center.

Mabel went over to Kassidy, "you okay?"

"Yeah, I'm fine," Kassidy stood up with Mabel's help.

Mabel looked at Jim, "if we attack the police, we do become the criminals the city thinks we are. There is another way out of this."

Codie nodded, "I agree. There is another way."

Jim chuckled, "of course you would take Mabel's side, just like what Andrew said about the race. Just because she helped you design the armor, you are sweet towards her."

Jim spat at Codie's feet. Codie shook his head again and marched up to Jim. He didn't touch him but stared into his eyes.

"Mabella has worked hard to form this community even before you knew what it was. So yes I value her opinion, but I don't favor her over anyone else," Codie turned around the circle, so he looked into every leaders' eyes, "and we need more time to come up with a good plan. So we will go calmly back to our lives and not do anything drastic, right?"

The leaders mumbled their agreement, and everyone started filing out of the room.

**Vital Era Container – 2:02 a.m.**

"You know that's two cabs in one night, don't you think we're pushing our luck?" Kay asked.

The team stood outside their container in the dark junkyard, with only their phones' flashlights to guide them. Mabel worked on getting the padlock of the doors open as the others watched her do it. Mabel had remained solemn after the meeting, and her teammates were concerned about what was said. She opened the doors and stepped back. Their flashlights illumined the inside.

Mabel looked at the others, "I want us to take everything out."

Will became confused, "why?"

Mabel let out a sigh, "I want us to take everything out like we aren't coming back to it. Does everyone understand?"

Everyone nodded, and Jericho shrugged his shoulders. But everyone went inside and started packing up everything. Will took care of the laptop, Baylor and Jericho rolled the scooter and bike out from the side of the container, and Kay started putting everything in the trunk. They worked fast.

Mabel helped Kay pull the heavy trunk out; they pulled it onto the dirt road. After that, the container was empty and free of their stuff, with the cot and table collapsed into smaller items and placed by the scooter. Will and Jericho closed the doors.

"Okay, you three are going to take home the little stuff along with our scooter and bike," Mabel pointed to Kay, "we are going to take this trunk home with the motorcycle. You wait here, while I go get it."

"Wait," Baylor stopped her, "you can't make us clean out the container, like this is the end, without any explanation."

Will was filled with shock, "is this the end?"

They all looked to Mabel with questioning looks. She gazed back and shook her head.

"I don't know," Mabel confessed, "but I know there won't be any games for a while. And something isn't right, and I want us to be prepared for the worse."

"Worse than what has already happened?" Kay inquired.

"With what I saw in there, I think it's going to become a lot worse," Mabel looked at each of them, "and we need to be ready for the ending of the Draconis games, for that seems to be the path we are all tumbling down."

Everyone was silent as Mabel's words sunk in. The Draconis games were weakening, and now it had finally been said.

Kay smiled weakly, "okay, let's get our stuff out of here, and go to Ridder Mansion."

The boys nodded and got on the scooter and bike. They rode down the dark dirt road.

"Kay, will you stay here while I go get the motorcycle?" Mabel asked.

"Of course," Kay answered.

Mabel nodded and moved into the darkness.

# Chapter 14

**Midtown, September 28, 2090 – 1:02 p.m.**

The long yellow bus rumbled down the road in Midtown. The large group of students on board screamed and yelled as it continued on its way. Energy seemed to be spilling out the windows with how the Golden Sierra School's students were acting. They were all in their streets clothes, and it made them excited that they didn't have to be in their uniforms for an hour, and that they were going to the main shopping place of Palaco City. Nothing could bring them down.

Mabel didn't feel the same way, none of the Vital Era team did. The five of them sat in the back quietly, looking out the windows thinking of something else other than shopping. Jericho and Will sat together on a seat, Baylor and Mabel share a seat, and Kay sat by herself. The excitement didn't affect them, as they continued in silence.

The bus stopped at a stoplight. Kay looked out the window and stared at the shops on the street.

Will looked back at his friend, "why are you mad at Kay?"

Will turned his gaze to Jericho. Jericho gave him a funny look, before rolling his eyes.

"Why do you care?" Jericho asked.

Will made a weird face, "because when you two idiots don't get along its sucks for the rest of us."

"Really?" Jericho smirked. "Idiots? That's how you view us. Well, I guess it's a good thing I'm learning now how you feel about me now," Jericho sarcastically said.

Will smacked him on the back of the head.

"Ow," Jericho rubbed his head, "why did you do that?"

"That's how you stop an idiot from talking," Will pushed Jericho off the seat with his legs.

Jericho fell hard onto the bus's floor, but only the Vital Era team noticed because the noises from the other students covered it up.

"You okay Jericho?" Baylor stood up from his seat.

"Yeah I'm fine," Jericho stood up and gave Will a mean look, "I think I'll change seats."

Will smirked and Baylor sat down, as Jericho moved to sit by Kay. She watched him casually as he seated himself.

"Did you two have a falling out?" she said snarkily.

Jericho sighed, "well you know Will, he thinks everything should be fine."

Kay nodded and went back to looking out the window. Jericho looked out the window too.

"I'm sorry if I hurt your feelings," he whispered to her.

She turned her attention back to him, "why?"

Jericho's face showed his confusion, "why? Because I'm sorry."

Kay shook her head, "are you just saying that because Will said to do it?"

Jericho rubbed the back of his head, "well I meant to say it, but Will wouldn't stop hitting me, so I thought it would be a good time to apologize."

"You're an idiot," Kay went to looking back out the window.

**Iron Mantel – 1:32 p.m.**

The students rushed off the bus and stampeded to the shops in the Compass Eye Outside Shopping Center that they had been brought too. The team was the last kids to get off, and the bus driver closed the doors behind them with a sigh of relief.

"What are we going to do?" Baylor asked.

No one responded.

"Okay," Baylor rubbed his chin, "maybe we should get something to eat, I mean I could go for anything right now."

Jericho smiled, "yeah that sounds good."

"Okay," Mabel agreed, "but I think I'll meet you guys there. I'm going to go visit Scott's place."

"Scott's place?" Jericho inquired.

"Yeah, he owns a shop called the Iron Mantel, they can repair anything from bicycles to small motorized vehicles," Kay explained.

Mabel waved goodbye and left the group as they went in search of a place to get food. She walked on the sidewalk, passing many shops until the Iron Mantel came into view. There were mechanical parts in the window and a sign that said open.

Mabel opened the door and went in. The shop was well organized with sections for bicycles and scooters. There was no one at the desk, so Mabel walked to the back of the store. She had been in the shop many times, and she knew where Scott would be if he wasn't in front.

She opened the door to the backroom. Inside were seven people. Each dressed in full glowing armor with their helmets on a table in the room.

"What?!" Mabel tried to back out, but the closest person grabbed her.

Mabel was pulled in and pushed into a chair. She stared at the people around her. They were all leaders of teams in the Draconis community. Scott, Andrew, Lacy, and Jim were some of them who surrounded her.

"What are you doing?" Mabel asked.

"Mabel, please listen to us," Scott pleaded, "we can't wait for Codie to think of something."

"It's not right!" Jim fumed.

"We are going to show the police, at their station, that they can't push us down," Lacy hissed.

Mabel shook her head, "this isn't right! Please don't do this; please rethink!"

Abbie, the team leader of Arch of Lily, spoke up, "I think we need to tie her down."

"No! Wait…" Mabel struggled against them, but they held her down.

"I got some rope over there," Scott timidly said.

Andrew grabbed it and wrapped it around Mabel, so she was tied to the chair.

"Look at what you are doing!" Mabel screamed.

"Get a gag!" Jim ordered.

Bram, the leader of the team Secret, grabbed duct tape from off the table. He ripped a piece off and placed it over Mabel's mouth, "that will keep her quiet."

"Good," Jim picked up his helmet, "let's get going."

**Compass Eye Outside Shopping Center – 1:43 p.m.**

Mabel struggled against the chair and rope. She wiggled as much as she could until finally, her chair tipped over. She landed hard on the floor with a big thud. But she didn't stop moving. The duct tape muffled her voice, and all she could do was mumble. She felt trapped and helpless.

Someone at the front of the shop tried to open the door but found it lock. Mabel could hear then trying to get in, but the person eventually gave up. Mabel shook her head and let out a sigh. Her hope was draining out, and a feeling of dread was starting to consume her.

But Mabel's helplessness didn't last long. The exit door which the team leaders had taken to the outside, opened. The light from the outside made it impossible to see who it was, but they walked in and hurried over to Mabel. When the door closed, she looked up into the face of her brother.

"What happened?" Will ripped the duct tape off of her mouth.

"Teams have gone rogue!" Mabel screamed.

Will's eyes widen with shock, "that's bad."

Mabel struggled against the rope as Will untied her from the chair. Finally released from her bonds, Mabel stood up.

"Where are the others?" Mabel asked.

The two of them rushed out the exit door, and back into the shopping compound. They ran around the building to the front.

"At a pretzel shop," Will answered, he started leading her towards them.

"We need to regroup," Mabel looked at the parking lot, "and we need a ride."

Will stopped, causing Mabel to turn towards him.

"We don't do that anymore," Will became terrified at Mabel suggestion.

"Will," Mabel gave her brother her full attention, "I know I promised we would never go down that path again. But a taxi won't get here fast enough, and we need to go now. They are going to attack the police station."

Mabel paused, "if we don't want to suffer another loss in disownment, or death. We must go, now!"

Will thought for a second before nodding, "I'll go get the others, find a car."

Will ran down the sidewalk. Leaving Mabel standing there, looking out at the parking lot. The lot was full of cars, shining in the sunlight, glistening like gold in a dragon's lair.

Mabel shook her head, "I hate this…I hate this!"

She screamed the last words in frustration, before stepping off of the sidewalk and going into the dragon's lair to pick out her victim.

"I guess we are criminals," Mabel mumbled to herself.

**Police Station – 2:17 p.m.**

Mabel drove through the streets of Palaco city in a rush. She continued to pass several cars along the way. Baylor, Jericho, and Will sat in the back of the stolen car, while Kay was in the passenger seat. It hadn't been easy to take the car, but after breaking the driver's window, Mabel had been able to start it.

"Will, have you contacted Codie?" Mabel went around a van in a flash.

"I'm calling him right now," Will sat in-between the two brothers as he held his cell phone to his ear, "it's ringing."

Will started talking quietly on the phone.

Jericho leaned forward in his seat, "should we call for the other teams?"

Kay turned to look at him, "and ask them to do what? I don't even know why we are following them, or why we are in a stolen car?!"

Mabel focused on the road, "we have to try and stop them before they attack. They aren't thinking right."

Will closed his phone, "Codie already knows."

"What?! How?!" Mabel asked as she turned a corner and the police station finally came into view.

There were people in glowing armored suits all over the street in front of the station, and police were everywhere trying to defend their building. The station was a square building which sometimes got mistaken for the library or the daycare center down the street. There were cops in their blue uniforms coming out of it.

Mabel stopped the car in the middle of the road, as the entire Vital Era team stared in shock at the scene before them. The armored people were beating the cops up, there were several bloody individuals, with a few of them already on the ground unconscious. Not one of the armored individuals used their light weapons; this was all hand to hand combat. But the cops were about to have a change of luck.

Two police officers stood on the roof of their square building and took out a special gun, that didn't fire bullets but magnetic waves that disrupted power in any object like the weapons the Draconis games used. The two officers turned the gun on and aimed it at the battlefield.

"What is that?" Baylor leaned so he could see through the front window.

The gun was fired as if to answer his question. The invisible blast went across the field, hitting the very edge of it. Several armored people lost power in their suits, along with Mabel and her team losing power in their car.

"Everyone out!" Mabel freaked out.

The police officers on the roof continued to fire their magnetic wave gun, as Vital Era scrambled to get out. Mabel pushed her team into an alley, as the war on the street continued to rage.

**Penguin Alley – 2:29 p.m.**

Codie ran down one of the alleys and onto the battle scene going on in the street. He could hardly believe his eyes at the actions of both sides. There were cops covered in blood, and there were several armored people on the ground being arrested. Both sides of the battlefield were losing people.

"What the heck?" he whispered to himself.

He stayed in the alley, not wanting to get mixed up in the battle, watching the chaos as it continued to rage around the area in the forms of punches and magnetic waves. Until his eyes caught something, he found Vital Era in the mix of it all. They stood scared in an alley watching the scene unfold in front of them.

"Crap," Codie said and without a second thought, rushed into the street.

He ducked and weaved between fighting individuals. Codie tried to avoid everyone, but someone had seen him enter the street. An officer followed him through the fights and caught up with him. She grabbed his arm and quickly brought down a handcuff on his wrist.

Codie turned around sharply, and before the cop could say anything, he pushed her away.

"You little..." she charged back at him and threw a punch.

Her fist smashed into Codie's eye, and he stumbled backward, falling onto the ground. The officer stood over him.

"Now, Codie Wright you are under arrest," she smiled.

Codie chuckled as he looked up, "funny, I don't remember giving my name out."

Before the officer could finish handcuffing him, Codie kicked her legs out from under her. She went down easy, giving him time to get away. Codie ran through the crowd without looking back. A black eye started forming on his face, but he didn't care.

He made it to Vital Era.

Mabel looked at him in surprise, "Codie?"

Her eyes were teary, as fear was setting in. Codie looked at the entire team and saw the same expression from them.

"Let's get out of here," he ordered, with a soft push to Baylor and Kay to move down the alley.

"But shouldn't we do something?" Jericho asked.

Codie placed a hand on Jericho's shoulder, "we can't do anything. We can't help the cops or even stop our people. We just need to leave the area," Codie looked back at the chaos, "before we get pulled into it."

The team started down the alley, leaving the station behind. They rushed down it, and away from the fighting.

"Our community was never violent," Mabel whispered, tears fell down her face.

Codie grabbed her hand and led her as Mabel's vision blurred from her tears.

# Chapter 15

Codie continued to lead the way back to Midtown, and away from the police station. The others followed him like sheep, not wanting to think.

"Where do you guys need to go?" he asked them.

Baylor gave him a glazed-over look, "we can go back to school. The bus driver didn't count how many kids there were; I doubt he'll count when the others get back on."

Codie nodded and led the team onto a new street. They walked casually. Codie had removed the handcuffs that had been placed on his wrist, but he couldn't do anything about the black eye forming on his face.

"I can't believe they would do that?" Kay whispered.

Jericho walked next to her; he placed an arm over her shoulders, "maybe we shouldn't be a part of it anymore?"

"But," Will shook his head, "that wasn't us...that wasn't our community."

"Then who was it?" Baylor looked at the younger boy, "come on Will. There's no denying who was fighting."

Mabel looked up from her place in the back and turned her attention to Codie. He still led the group.

"Codie?" Mabel watched him stop and turn around, "how did you know so quickly that the fight was going on?"

The group stopped and waited for his answer.

"Joi told me," he informed them.

"Oh," Mabel tilted her head, "how did she know?"

Codie shrugged his shoulders, "one of the team members told her about the planning of the fight, and by that, she was able to conclude when and where it was going to happen, I guess."

"Okay," Mabel nodded slowly, unsure of the truth.

The group went back to walking. Cars passed them by, and people on the sidewalk went by them without a word.

Codie stopped again, everyone gave him a funny look, "I want to say something."

He looked behind his shoulder before going into an alleyway for privacy. The team followed.

"I want you all to know that people in our community don't agree with what happened. When people hear about this, they are going to be outraged by those teams," Codie explained to them.

Mabel looked around at her team before speaking, "and what do you want us to do? Is everyone in the fight today banned, what if their leaders told them to fight, or told them you had ordered it? What is going to happen?"

Codie shook his head, "right now, I think there are people who are going to be banned because of today, but for those who didn't get caught by the cops, they will have to answer to me."

**Meditation Classroom, October 2, 2090 – 8:20 a.m.**

Students that were late, filed into the meditation classroom without a worry. The professor never moved from his yoga mat. Jericho and Baylor were one of the last students to enter. The rest of the team was waiting for them in their usual spots on the ground. Will, Kay, and Mabel greeted them as they sat down on their mats. But before any words could be said between them, the speaker system in the school came to life.

"Attention students!" it yelled to the entire school, "we have some local news we would like to inform you about."

Kay shared a look with Jericho, but no one said a word as they waited for the news.

"In the past few days, there has been violence in our city from the local motorcycle gang that has been plaguing us for years now. There have been many arrests, and now the police are coming to us for help. If anyone knows where a man named Codie Wright is, please inform the police right away," the speakers announced, "sorry teachers for the interruption. Please have a good school day."

The news made the classroom erupt in chatter, the news had been on the TV but having the school announce it, made it even more fascinating.

Vital Era looked at each other as the news sunk in.

"How did they get his name?" Will asked.

"I didn't even know his full name," Baylor mumbled.

Mabel shook her head, "that's insane."

Kay looked at Mabel, "you're right. There is someone going rogue in the games."

The boys gave them strange looks.

"When did this become a possibility?" Will asked.

"Isn't that jumping to a conclusion," Jericho shrugged his shoulders, "I mean couldn't it have been someone who got arrested."

"No," Mabel rubbed her chin, "everyone knew his first name, but very few knew his last name. It could have come from one of the people arrested, but it is more likely someone who hasn't been arrested because they might be working with the police."

"Okay," Will agreed, "that makes some sense. But who would be doing this? Andrew, or Jim?"

"No, not them. They just recently lost people," Kay pointed out.

"Then who?" Baylor asked.

"Well," Mabel started counting on her fingers, "we know Codie's name, his team knows his name, the Magic know his name, the Spells know it, and the Storms know it."

"And the Spells was one of the teams that attacked the station," Kay said, "could it be them?"

Mabel shrugged her shoulders, "don't know. They didn't get arrested, but that could mean something or nothing."

**Lunchroom – 12:09 p.m.**

The lunchroom was crowded and noisy as usual; no one seemed to be acting differently after the announcement that morning, even the Vital Era team was trying to be normal.

Will laid his head on the lunch table. He let out a sigh, as he pushed his food tray away. Kay sat next to him, picking at her food with a plastic fork.

"I wish they would give us edible food," Kay mumbled.

Jericho walked up to the table with a juice box, "Baylor and Mabel are behind me."

Kay nodded, before eyeing his juice box suspiciously, "where's your food?"

Jericho pulled his juice closer to himself, "I'm not getting any food today, just juice for me."

Kay smirked, "lucky."

Mabel and Baylor walked up, and each took a seat at the table. Their food was just as unrecognizable.

"It amazes me," Baylor started, "how stupid people can be."

Kay gave Baylor a tired look, and Jericho smirked at his brother. Will didn't raise his head from the table.

"Why?" Kay asked half-heartedly.

"You know Sammie," Baylor looked over his friends' heads and to the other side of the lunchroom, "well, Craig convinced him that chocolate milk comes from special cows."

Mabel chuckled, and Kay just shook her head.

A young man walked briskly towards them; he wore one of the school's uniforms even though it didn't fit properly. He was too big for it, making it a hazard, as the buttons looked like they were ready to pop off. The man sat down by Will.

Will sat up and looked at the young man, "oh, hey Jeb. What brings you to our school?"

"Nice uniform," Kay smiled at him.

Jeb gave Kay a funny look, "I was wondering if you guys could help Codie out?"

"Sure," Mabel responded, "what do you need?"

"A place to hide him," Jeb explained.

Baylor and Jericho both shared a look.

"Where are we going to put him?" Baylor asked, "it's not like we can put him in the dorms."

Mabel thought for a moment, "true…what about the Ridder Mansion?"

Kay considered it, "it's not like he can go inside, but he could hang out behind the walls for a couple of days. It's where we have our stuff right now anyway. So I guess so."

"That sounds good," Jeb took out his phone and started texting.

"Why does Codie need help?" Jericho asked.

Jeb didn't look up from his phone, "those who have been arrested have ratted out all of his hiding places, and the community's places as well. The containers got raided."

Jeb looked up, "but no worries about that. Most everyone, like you guys, knew better than to keep their stuff there after the meeting."

Jeb got up from the table, and he walked away.

**Ridder Mansion – 12:36 p.m.**

Jericho, Baylor, Will, Kay, and Mabel looked both ways before crossing the street. They hurried to the other side, to Ridder Mansion. The team made it to the driveway and walked to where their stuff was being stored. Everything was under blankets, so if someone wandered in, they wouldn't see it right a way.

"Thanks for letting me stay here," Codie said from behind them, he was on the other side of the driveway.

His comment made the group jump, before turning around to see him. He still had his torn leather jacket on, but his black eye was almost healed.

"Hey Codie," Jericho greeted, "don't scare us like that."

Codie gave them a funny look, "sorry didn't mean to."

Jeb peeked from around him, he was still in the school's uniform, "but it was really funny watching you guys jump like mice."

Mabel walked over to Codie and gave him a hug, "how are you holding up?"

They released the embrace.

"I'm fine," Codie gestured to behind his shoulder, "but if Kassidy hadn't found me before the cops, this would be a different story."

The team looked behind Codie and saw Kassidy sitting against a wall, listening to a police scanner with headphones. They turned their attention back to Codie.

"Why didn't your team help you?" Kay asked.

"They are helping other teams out right now," Codie rubbed the back of his head, "Winfred is with the Travelers, and Gayla and Lali are talking with the Knights."

Will tilted his head, "but the Knights were caught, weren't they?"

Codie agreed, "yes, but during this time, some of the rules are being bent, to try and save the games."

"And this won't hurt us," Baylor inquired, "if we contact someone who might be on the police's radar?"

Codie shook his head, "I think the police are overwhelmed right now with the recent teams they've caught. An old one won't be their priority."

"What about Joi?" Kay asked.

"She's doing her own thing right now," Codie answered.

Jeb looked around the group.

He smiled, "would any of you guys have any food on you?"

"Yeah," Jericho pulled out a protein bar and handed it over to Jeb.

Jeb nodded, "thanks."

Jeb took the bar and walked over to Kassidy to sit by her before he opened it up and started eating.

"Well," Mabel peeked over at the school, "I think you should be fine here, no one from the school comes over. And if anyone wanders in, their usually a drunk or something."

"Thanks again for helping me," Codie smiled.

Will, Jericho, and Kay waved goodbye and started walking back to school. Baylor and Mabel watched them go.

Mabel turned to Codie again, "do you know who gave your name to the cops?"

Codie scratched his chin, "no, but I'm working on finding out."

Mabel nodded and started walking to the school with Baylor. Codie watched them go.

**School Hallway – 12:48 p.m.**

The Vital Era team meandered down the hallway, the bell for the next period to start hadn't rung yet, so there was no reason to hurry.

"I wonder if the Knights will get to come back fully," Will stretched his arms, "that would be so good. I hope they do."

Mabel chuckled, "if we were completely legal, they could come back, everyone who got caught by the cops could come back, and we wouldn't be in the mess we're in now."

Kay and Jericho both gave Mabel a funny look.

"That doesn't seem realistic," Baylor pointed out.

Mabel got a determined look in her eyes, "you just haven't seen the possibilities."

"Okay," Kay put her hands up, "weird alert."

Mabel punched Kay in the arm, and the team laughed. But their laughter stopped when Denzil turned a corner and stood in front of them.

"I've been looking for you Ms. Overton," Denzil walked up to the group.

They all became quiet and serious as the principal of their school walked up to them in a rush.

"What's the matter Principal Denzil?" Mabel asked cautiously.

Denzil stopped right in front of the group and straightened her dress suit, "I need to talk to you about the man that visited you a couple of days ago. You said he was from your father's work?"

Mabel grew pale, "yes, I believe he had just started there, working as a mechanic."

Denzil nodded, "well, have you seen the news."

No one said anything.

Denzil continued, "they have been showing a picture on the news of a criminal the police are looking for in relation to the attack on the police station…I believe that the man they are looking for is the same one that came to you."

Mabel tried to keep herself calm, as everyone behind her filled with shock. Will nervously played with a button on his jacket.

"I don't think they are the same person," Mabel lied, "his name was Doyle."

Denzil eyed them with suspicion, "that's not a very common name. What was the man's first name? Arthur, like Sir Arthur Conan Doyle, perhaps?"

Mabel smiled nervously; Kay looked around as if looking for an escape. Baylor and Jericho didn't make eye contact with Denzil.

"That's funny," Mabel chuckled a little, "I hadn't realized he shared the same last name as the author of *Sherlock Holmes*, he probably gets that a lot. But his first name isn't Arthur; it's Jules."

Before Denzil could ask another question, the bell for the next period rang.

"Well, we got to go," Mabel announced.

The group rushed away from Denzil; she watched them run down the hallway, with her suspicion growing.

# Chapter 16

Baylor and Jericho sat at their desks in homeroom classroom. The point of homeroom was to get caught up on homework, but for the last few days, the news had become a part of it. There hadn't been another attack on the police station, but the police had managed to track down several individuals who were part of the Draconis community with the help of those arrested.

Jericho and Baylor watched the TV in their classroom, other kids watched it too, but some weren't interested anymore. A news reporter talked about the latest arrest. They showed on the screen the four people who had been caught.

Jericho looked at his brother, who sat behind him, and whispered, "that's the entire Viking team."

"Yeah that is, I can't believe they were caught," Baylor's face was covered with confusion, "it's just unbelievable."

"I wonder if the police caught them, or if someone ratted them out?" Jericho looked back at the TV.

"You think someone would have ratted them out?" Baylor leaned forward, so their conversation could stay between them.

Jericho nodded slightly, "I would if I had followed them into attacking the police station and then got caught. I would have sold them out in a minute."

Baylor gave his brother a questioning look, "remind me never to double-cross you."

Jericho shrugged his shoulders "it's simply logical to consider. Jim was one of the main leaders being aggressive. I won't be shocked if other teams like the Seals or Camo get taken down next. They would be the next ones I would go after."

Baylor thought for a moment, "I guess we'll have to wait and see. But if it's a team not part of the attack, what would that say about the person snitching on the community?"

Jericho turned to look at his brother, "why would it say anything different?"

Baylor leaned even closer to his brother, "well, what if you were the individual trying to take the games down. I wouldn't go after the teams that attacked. I would go after ones who didn't, so to create a bigger divide among us."

"That's true," Jericho turned back around, "we will have to wait and see what happens next. This will be a defining moment for everyone."

The teacher in the classroom stood up from her chair and walked over to the TV, she turned it off and faced the class, "time for you all to work on homework or read."

The teacher went back to her desk and sat down; she picked up the book she had been reading. Baylor and Jericho both pulled out homework to work on, ending their conversation.

**Hallway – 1:36 p.m.**

Jericho and Baylor left their homeroom and started making their way through the crowded hallways of school. Students rushed around trying to get to their next classes, even though there were five minutes. The boys continued to walk through the crowd at a leisurely pace. Until a hand grabbed Jericho on the shoulder, the brothers turned.

Kay, the one gripping Jericho's shoulder, pulled them to the side of the hallway so they wouldn't be in anyone's way. Mabel came up behind Kay and joined them.

"Hey," Baylor greeted, "did you see the news?"

"Yes," Mabel said.

"Crazy," Kay commented, "but that's not why we are here."

"What's up?" Jericho inquired.

"Kassidy was able to pick up on the scanner, that our spot," Mabel informed, "at Ridder Mansion, has been put on their radar as a place Codie might be."

Shock filled the brothers at the news. The Viking team getting caught wasn't completely unexpected, but Ridder Mansion being found out was.

"Do we need to get him out of there now?" Jericho asked.

"No," Mabel answered.

"It's not high on their list," Kay looked around at the rushing students, "they will eventually get to it though, but right now they have other things they need to look into first."

"Okay, but what do we need to do?" Baylor asked.

"Well," Mabel rubbed the back of her neck, "we need to go find a new place for him to hide."

"Why do we need to do that?" Jericho gave her a funny look.

"Because his team is tied up with others," Mabel explained, "so that leaves us. Will can't do it because he has a test next period, and Kay can't miss another class period right now. I can go, but I was wondering if one of you could help me?"

Baylor smiled, "sure, I can help. I have an art class next, so it's no problem."

"That sounds good," Mabel smiled back at him.

The girls were about to leave, but Jericho stopped them.

"Wait, what do you think you're going to do? Look online for places to hide a criminal?" Jericho asked.

Mabel shrugged her shoulders, "I don't know. Right now I was thinking of just visiting parts of the city to see if any place looked good. There are several abandoned buildings in Cashe Corner."

Jericho shook his head, "don't take him to Cashe Corner, that place is a hot spot, and any sign of Codie will be instantly reported."

Mabel nodded, "okay, that makes sense, then we'll avoid Cashe Corner and try to find a place that doesn't get a lot of attention."

"Sounds good," Baylor waved goodbye, "we'll see you guys later."

Mabel and Baylor walked down the hallway together.

**Bayside Point – 2:41 p.m.**

Baylor rode the dirt bike down the road, and Mabel held on to him as she looked around for any useful buildings. They had both changed out of their school uniforms so they wouldn't look so suspicious driving around. This section of Palaco city had several businesses and homes; it seemed to be a combination of a residential and shopping areas. So they would pass houses, then a couple of businesses would interrupt the chain of homes before going back to houses.

"I don't think we will find anything in this section," Mabel told Baylor.

Baylor pulled the bike over to the side, so the two of them could talk.

"Well, we could go search somewhere else, but I don't think we've given this place enough of a chance," Baylor looked at Mabel over his shoulder.

"I guess," Mabel sighed.

"What's up?" Baylor turned around to look at her.

"I don't know," Mabel shook her head, "all of this is just so much. And I think I'm growing tired of it."

Baylor frowned, "I'm shocked we've stayed for as long as we have."

Mabel looked at him, "there's a reason for that… Codie was there for us when we needed a helping hand."

Baylor tilted his head, "what do you mean?"

A car passed by them, but they didn't notice it.

"We started working for Codie about a year ago," Mabel explained, "but we knew him a year before that. He caught us trying to steal his car."

"So that wasn't your first time at the Compass shopping center?" Baylor asked.

Mabel shook her head, "no…we started stealing cars after my mother went into a coma…it happened after a car accident."

Tears started going down Mabel's face. Baylor kicked out the kickstand and got off the bike. He embraced Mabel.

"I had no idea," he whispered to her.

Mabel cried into Baylor's shoulder, "she passed away over the summer, after two years of being in a coma."

The two continued to embrace each other for several minutes before they released the embrace.

"That's why," Mabel continued her explanation, "we have been working so hard to keep this community alive. We built it with Codie. When he found us, all he had was an idea, then we brought our own skill set…and a few months later the games was developed."

"Wow," Baylor whispered.

Baylor smiled, and got back on the bike, putting the kickstand back in place, "then let's continue to look. We haven't covered this area completely."

They rode back onto the street and started their search again for a building that could help them in their mission.

**Coloris Lapides Gym – 3:17 p.m.**

Baylor and Mabel rode down a road in the middle of Bayside Point. They still hadn't had any luck in finding a place. It was almost time for them to move on to a different section of the city.

Mabel looked down at her phone, and examined the map of the area, "hey can you take a right, at the next light?"

Baylor nodded, "sure."

Baylor rode the bike to the stoplight and turned right. The new street had businesses on it and no homes.

"Could we go a couple feet, and when you see the Mystery Bakery, stop," Mabel ordered.

Baylor rode the bike down the street until the bakery came into view, he pulled over to the side of the road, letting a car pass them.

"What now?" Baylor looked over his shoulder at Mabel.

She looked up from her phone, "well, there should be an old gym here, from the college, called Coloris Lapides, and I was thinking we could look at it."

Mabel got off the bike and looked at her phone one last time before putting it back in her pocket. Baylor turned the bike off and kicked out its kickstand. The two of them walked down the sidewalk until the building they were looking for came into view.

It was an old looking building. The old gym was huge, and it looked like it could hold a football field in it. There appeared to be three levels, and several windows. The doors at the front were made of glass with a few cracks. The square brick building looked like it had been abandoned for years, with an old for sale sign on the front of it.

"It's perfect," Mabel smiled.

"Really?" Baylor tilted his head as he continued to look at the rundown building, "it's a project."

"Well, that's one of the ways its perfect," Mabel smiled at Baylor before running up to the building, "I mean look at how big it is!"

Baylor walked up to the building, while Mabel looked in through one of the glass doors. He sighed.

"Well, are we going to break in?" he asked.

Mabel shook her head, "no."

She looked at the for sale sign and took out her phone. She dialed the number on it. It rang.

"Hello," Mabel greeted, "I was wondering how much money for the old gym in Bayside Point?... Really that much? Okay, I will be in contact with you."

Mabel hung up the phone and hugged Baylor. He returned the embrace with surprise written all over his face.

"Why are we hugging?" he inquired.

"The payment is reasonable," Mabel released Baylor, "and the down payment is ten thousand dollars…We can get this building."

**Ridder Mansion – 3:56 p.m.**

The dirt bike touched the driveway of Ridder Mansion as Baylor and Mabel returned from their travels around the city. Mabel jumped off the bike, while Baylor parked it behind the wall. She rushed over to Codie, who sat on the other side of the driveway watching them.

"We found a great place!" she exclaimed.

Codie remained sitting against the wall, while he watched her with a smile, "you did? That was quick."

Baylor, after putting the blanket over their stuff, walked over to the two of them, "we did, it was the last street in Bayside Point we looked at."

Codie stood up, "okay, well tell me about it."

"It's the old college's gym that they no longer use, Coloris Lapides…and I own it now," Mabel informed Codie.

Codie frowned, "what do you mean you own it? You've only been gone for an afternoon; how could you already own the building?"

"Well, I called the number on the for sale sign and said I would be interested," Mabel started explaining, "and as Baylor was driving us back here, I got another phone call from them. They wanted us to make an offer because it appears that the building has been on the market for a few years, and the owners didn't want it anymore. So I was able to make the down payment for ten thousand dollars, and now the building is mine."

Mabel beamed with happiness at her find. Baylor just shook his head and smiled at his friend's energy. Codie gave the two of them a nod and rubbed his chin as he thought about what Mabel had said.

"Well, that sounds good. What are you planning on doing next?" Codie asked.

"We were going to take all our stuff there along with you," Mabel gestured to their items on the other side of the driveway, "and then maybe start fixing the place up. It's going to need some work."

Codie nodded again, "okay, I like the sound of it. I can start taking some of your stuff over there if you want, but I won't be able to do that until night time."

"That's okay, Kassidy said we should have a day to clear out," Mabel said, "so we can wait till tonight to transfer everything over, besides the owners are mailing me the key today, and it should be in my box at the post office, so we can't get in until the keys arrive."

"They didn't want to meet you?" Codie asked.

"Oh, they no longer live here. The owners live in a different state, but the keys should get here tonight, they're expressing them the whole way," Mabel informed Codie.

"Well, okay…we have a building," Codie smiled a crooked smile.

# Chapter 17

Mabel's history professor, Fletcher, walked in front of the class holding a textbook. Every student had a copy of the same book on their desks. The class was reading aloud from one of the pages in the book. The civil war was just ending, and Abraham Lincoln was about to be killed.

"One thing we should know about this period," Fletcher started, "is that Abraham Lincoln and John Wilkes Booth both had several pictures taken of them before Booth killed Lincoln, which was very rare during that time because of the cameras they had, and how long it took to take a picture."

A student raised his hand, and Professor Fletcher looked to him.

"Yes, Mr. Bing?" Fletcher held his book with one hand.

"Why was Booth photographed so much?" the student asked.

Fletcher closed his book, "that's because he was an actor. It's also the reason he was allowed into the theater the night he killed Lincoln. He blended in with the stagehands because he worked there. No one questioned his presence."

"So no one saw it coming?" the same student asked.

"Right, Mr. Bing," Fletcher praised.

Fletcher opened his book back up and turned to the page his class was on, but before he could start his lecture again. Mrs. Stevenson came into the room with a police officer.

"Professor Fletcher, I'm sorry to interrupt your class, but we need a moment," Mrs. Stevenson announced.

Fletcher frowned, "what is this about?"

The officer remained quiet as Mrs. Stevenson walked up to Fletcher.

"I need to escort Mabella Overton to the office," Mrs. Stevenson explained.

"Why?" Fletcher closed his book again, "we're in the middle of class, can't this wait."

"No sir, we need her now," the officer responded.

"Really? She shouldn't be missing class; she'll fall behind," Fletcher eyed the officer suspiciously.

"This can't wait," the officer answered.

Fletcher became furious, "fine! But I want to see her back before class ends!"

Mrs. Stevenson walked over to Mabel, who had been listening quietly to their conversation.

"Ms. Overton, could you please come with me? Bring your stuff," Mrs. Stevenson directed.

Mabel started packing up her stuff, with a glance towards the officer. Her stomach was uneasy, and she felt like sweat was dripping from her forehead.

"Ms. Overton," Fletcher glared at the officer, "the reading for this week will be chapters ten through twelve."

"Okay Professor Fletcher," Mabel finished putting away her things and stood up from her desk.

With her backpack in hand, she walked to the back of the class with Mrs. Stevenson escorting her. They went out the door, and the officer followed them out.

**Front Office – 8:36 a.m.**

Mrs. Stevenson and the officer walked Mabel down the hall and to the front office. In the front office were her other teammates. Will, Kay,

Jericho, and Baylor all in their school's uniforms, and all sitting in seats against the wall by Principal Denzil's office. They looked as nervous as her.

"Please sit there," Mrs. Stevenson pointed to a seat next to Will.

Mabel sat down. Will, gave her a worried look and the two of them locked hands. Mrs. Stevenson and the officer walked into Denzil's office and went in; an argument could be heard going on inside. Angry voices drifted from it but stopped when the door closed.

Mabel turned to her friends and teammates, "what's going on?"

Baylor, at the end of the row of seats, turned, so he faced them, "a detective is here for us."

Kay shook her head, "they can't know anything, there's nothing on us."

"Or maybe we've been ratted on," Jericho whispered.

The team all turned their attention to him, as he looked at the floor quietly. Baylor put his arm on Jericho's shoulders.

"We were talking about that," Baylor mumbled, "that we thought a team, who didn't attack the police station, would be the next team to get arrested…I guess we were right."

Kay sighed and grabbed one of Jericho's hands and squeezed it tight, "don't worry, we won't go to jail."

Jericho looked at Kay and gave a small smile. Baylor released his brother and stood up, stretching his arms.

"Why would we be targeted?" Will mumbled.

Mabel looked at her brother, "I think how close we are to Codie made us a target. That's all I can think of for that question."

Baylor approved, "I agree, it would make sense to try and take us out to weaken Codie."

Someone shouted in the office, and Baylor turned his gaze to the door. He frowned at it, as the yelling stopped.

"I wonder what Denzil is doing?" Baylor rubbed the back of his neck, "I mean what does she expect to do. Keep us from the officers."

"Well," Mabel sighed, "I might have forgotten some little piece of info about Denzil and the connection to our family."

Baylor's face became annoyed, "she's not your aunt, is she?"

Mabel shook her head, "no, but Denzil knew our mom well. There's a reason we haven't been expelled...Denzil was a very close friend to our mom."

Shock filled Baylor, "seriously, that's why you have been able to sneak out so many times. She pities you guys…I should have guessed."

"True," Jericho became interested in the news, "we should have known something was up."

Their conversation ended as Denzil opened the door to her office, "I need you five to come in."

**Denzil's Office – 8:42 a.m.**

The five of them walked into the office. Denzil and Mrs. Stevenson were the only individuals from the school in the room. Two officers, including the one who had escorted Mabel, and a detective were in the room as well. The officers wore their blue uniforms, while the detective wore a red pantsuit. She had long wavy blonde hair, and her skin had a coco tone to it. Her face was very beautiful. She sat in Denzil's seat, and Denzil seemed to be peeved by it.

"Will you all please sit down," the detective gestured to the seats in front of Denzil's desk, there happened to be five of them.

They all sat down, while all the adults, except the detective, stayed standing.

"Good morning, I'm Detective Esmaralda Shepard,' Shepard introduced herself.

No one responded.

"Okay," Shepard placed her elbows on the desk, "do you students remember the attack that happened to the police station about a week ago?"

"Yes," Kay looked into Shepard's eyes, "we all saw it on the news."

Shepard nodded slowly, "well, some of those individuals have been giving us info about their gang...and several of them have talked about a team called Vital Era...would you know anything about that?"

Will kept his head down, while Jericho stared at the desk without making any eye contact. Baylor straightened himself in his seat and Kay continued to look defiantly into Shepard's eyes.

Mabel tilted her head, "I can't say that I have ever heard those terms put together, I truly don't think any of us have."

Shepard squinted her eyes, "they also say you recently got new teammates, can you explain why the Alans have suddenly started hanging out with the three of you?"

Shepard gestured to Jericho and Baylor. Jericho didn't move, but Baylor turned his head to Mabel, he didn't know what to say.

"Okay," Mabel put her hands in the air, "the truth is Jericho and Kay are dating."

Will, Jericho, and Kay both looked sharply to Mabel, with complete shock on their faces. Kay and Jericho still held each other's hands. Baylor smiled and suppressed a laugh.

"Yeah," Mabel put her hands down, "they didn't want to be public about it because Kay is shy. And Baylor started coming along because he was just a bonus to Jericho…there's really nothing else going on."

Shepard continued to eye the five of them suspiciously, "well isn't that convenient."

"Not really," Mabel continued, "being around lovebirds is very annoying, sometimes I wish they were in a different school."

Mabel smiled at Shepard, but it didn't sway her. Shepard stood up from the desk.

"We are taking these five students to the police station," Shepard told Denzil.

Denzil gritted her teeth but nodded. Shepard walked out of the office and the officers went over to Mabel and her team, making them stand up.

**Golden Sierra School – 9:06 a.m.**

The officers escorted the Vital Era team out of the school. They walked through the front doors and onto the paved walkway. Mabel led the group, Kay was behind her, Jericho came next, Will after him, and Baylor at the end. The officers were at each end of their small little parade, while Denzil and Shepard walked ahead of the group talking very quickly to one another. The team felt like they were prisoners walking to their execution.

Mabel looked over her shoulder and saw that several students were watching them being escorted. They were in the windows, and there was a big group of them on the glass bridge. All of them wore their navy blue school uniforms, making it look like an infection was in the building.

Mabel turned her head back and focused on walking behind Denzil and Shepard. They were being led to the parking lot of Golden Sierra School. They turned the corner and continued their march.

Ridder Mansion was to their left, standing tall against the sunlight, and casting a shadow across the street. Will looked at the place. Codie wasn't there anymore, and Will wondered if he would try and stop the officers if he had been.

But there was no help from the mansion, and the team continued to the parking lot. A police van was waiting in the lot. The parade stopped right in front of the vehicle as Denzil and Shepard stopped to finish their conversation.

"So what, I'm supposed to wait for you to return my students, what should I tell their parents. That the police think they are part of an illegal gang in Palaco city, and the police are simply investigating them, don't worry!?" Denzil's anger was flaring, "you expect this to go well with the parents!?"

"Principal Denzil, they are simply going to be asked questions, they won't be accused of anything, and there will be a social worker at the station for them, you shouldn't have to contact their parents right away," Shepard started her official statement, "and we will contact their parents if anything arises, you don't need to worry."

Denzil's anger continued to rise, but she couldn't do anything about it. Shepard gestured to the officers, and they went to the van and opened up the side door. They filed the team into the van. Mabel and Kay sat in the back, while the boys shared the middle seat. The door to the van shut, and the team was locked in the vehicle.

"What should we do?" Will whispered.

Mabel leaned forward, "be as honest with them as you can, but don't say anything about the community. We can't give ourselves up yet."

Will went back to sitting quietly. Shepard walked over to her car, while the officers got into the van and started it up.

**Police Van – 9:13 a.m.**

Everyone was quiet as the van drove through the streets of Palaco City. The officers didn't say anything, while one of them drove and the other looked at the passing cars, and neither did Vital Era. It felt like the silence was keeping them in chains, making sure they couldn't get away. Will hung his head, and stared at his hands. Jericho stared ahead, as he sat in the middle of his brother and Will. Baylor looked out the window, watching the world pass them by. The girls in the back weren't much different from the boys. Mabel looked out her window, while Kay stared harshly at the officers.

Kay looked at Mabel, who still stared out her window, before leaning forward to Jericho. She placed a hand on his shoulder, he leaned back.

"Can you start talking to your brother or Will?" Kay whispered into his ear.

"Why?" he gave her a weird look.

"I need to talk to Mabel, but it's the stuff we don't want others to hear, okay?" Kay asked.

Jericho sighed, "hey Baylor, what's your favorite color?"

Jericho asked the question loud enough for everyone, and Kay to give him a weird look. But his brother shook his head and started the conversation.

Kay leaned back and turned her attention to Mabel, "do you think we should try contacting someone?"

Mabel watched Jericho and Baylor talk, "no."

The two girls talked quietly that even Will couldn't hear them.

"Why not?" Kay continued to eye the officers, "I don't think anyone knows we've been picked up."

"I don't think anyone knows either," Mabel moved her lips slowly, "but we can't tell anyone. We don't want to have another reason to attack the police station…so we should remain quiet."

Kay shook her head, "and what if they find us guilty, or they have great evidence against us? What then?"

Mabel sighed, "we go down."

Shock covered Kay's face, "really?  Just like that, not even a peep of protest?"

Mabel nodded, "Kay, we can't come at this and view ourselves as innocent, we broke the law.  And if they have that evidence on us, then so be it.  But if they don't, we live another day."

Kay slumped in her seat, "so that's just it.  The community will be dead to us…and what are we supposed to do after…play checkers in prison?"

Mabel shook her head, "I don't know, but we will take the consequences and deal with it.  This won't be an end for us, and this won't be an end for the games."

Mabel turned her head to Kay, "whatever happens we will work together, okay?"

# Chapter 18

Codie worked within the old gym. The inside of the gym wasn't as bad as the outside. There were cobwebs everywhere, but the structure had remained sound, and all the sections of the building had remained intact for the most part.

Sunlight filtered into the main gym through dirty windows at the top and danced on the old floor. Codie worked among the pools of dirty sunlight, sweeping up piles of dust. He had taken his leather jacket off, so his t-shirt and jeans were the only things to get dirty. Sweat dripped down his forehead, as he continued to pile the dust.

Ringing from his phone stopped his progress. The phone wasn't in the main gym but the front entrance. Codie let out a sigh, and walked to the side of the gym, putting his broom against a wall, and going through a door to the front entrance.

Vital Era's stuff was in the area. Their trunk, scooter, dirt bike, and modified motorcycle all occupied the area. Codie's stuff; his jacket, backpack and duffel bag, sat on the trunk and his phone rang from one of the jacket's pockets.

Codie picked up his jacket and started searching for his phone. The ringing continued to get louder until he got it out of one of the pockets. Taking it in hand, Codie answered it.

"Hello?" he greeted.

"Codie!" the voice said.

"Joi? Where have you been, I haven't seen you for a week," Codie sat down on the trunk while he talked.

"I was helping other teams," Joi explained.

"Right," Codie said slowly, "what's up?"

"Vital Era has been picked up by the cops," Joi informed him.

Codie removed the phone from his ear and looked at it. His stomach went sour, and he suddenly wanted to throw the phone.

Codie put the phone back to his ear, "how do you know?"

Joi didn't answer for several seconds, "one of the teams that attacked the police station saw them…I didn't think you would want to hear that from one of them…but I don't think they would make this up."

Codie rubbed his chin, "which team specifically?"

"Vikings," Joi answered promptly.

Codie stood up from the trunk and started pulling on his jacket, "and why would they suddenly help us, Joi? I thought they were still bitter."

"I don't know," Joi confessed, "but I don't think they would lie about this…they know how much Vital Era means."

The last statement took Codie by surprise. He took the phone from his ear again and turned it off while shaking his head. Codie put the phone in his pocket, pulled on his backpack, grabbed the dirt bike and pushed it out the front entrance of Coloris Lapides.

**Police Station, Holding Cells – 9:47 a.m.**

The holding cells in the police station were generic. Steel bars in square shapes, with cots and a toilet. The Vital Era team was placed into two cells next to each other. One for the boys and the other for the girls. Will and Jericho sat on one of the cots in their cell, while Baylor leaned against the bars, hanging his arms through them. Kay paced the girls' cell, while Mabel watched her go back and forth from one of the cots.

"How long have we been in here?" Will asked.

Mabel looked over at her brother, "like five minutes, what clock are you on?"

Will sighed and leaned his back on the bars, "it's just felt like longer to me. These cells are very screwy with my senses."

Jericho gave him a weird look, "senses, what are you a werewolf or something?"

Kay didn't stop pacing as she answered, "if he was, I'm pretty sure we would have noticed by now."

Baylor shook his head, "well, we didn't know you and Jericho were dating."

That stopped Kay's pacing, as she ran to their side of the cell and stuck her arms through the bars, trying to get Baylor, "I'm going to make you pay for that comment!"

Baylor didn't move, but gave her a weird look, "I'm not the one who made it up, Mabel is."

Kay stopped reaching through the bars and turned slowly to Mabel. Mabel watched with amusement on her face, as her friend started to inch closer.

"Why are you giving me that look?" Mabel asked.

Kay continued to get closer, "because you are going to pay for the lies!"

Kay jumped towards Mabel, but slammed into Mabel's foot, as she had raised it to defend herself against the attack. The two then fell to the floor and started wrestling. Jericho and Will watched from their cot, while Baylor glanced at them before staring back at the wall.

"Why do you two always wrestle, I mean I don't even wrestle with Jericho, and we're brothers?" Baylor asked.

The girls stopped their playing around and sat on the ground.

"Because that's how we bond," Kay stood up, "I mean, I'm not one for movies and popcorn, but some people bond that way. I like to wrestle and tackle someone…it just who I am."

Mabel still sat on the floor, "yeah, it took us a while to get used to it in the beginning."

Their conversation ended as two police officers, and Detective Shepard came to the holding cells. She pointed to Jericho and Mabel.

"I want those two, and put each of them in an interrogation room," Shepard ordered.

**Interrogation Room – 10:02 a.m.**

Mabel sat down behind a table. She faced the one-way mirror and watched her reflection in it. She knew Jericho was in a similar room down the hall. Mabel sat quietly in the room waiting for someone to come in. The room itself wasn't anything glamorous, just cream paint for the walls, and black carpet on the floor.

The door to the interrogation room opened, and Detective Shepard walked in with a file in hand. Her red pantsuit was still looking fresh and nice, even with the day's activities. She sat down on the other side of the table and opened up the file. There appeared to be text on the modified motorcycles, and members of the community. Mabel watched Shepard sift through them.

"Don't I need my dad here?" Mabel asked.

Shepard didn't look up from her papers, "you and Jericho Alan are both eighteen years old. You are by law an adult. The two of you don't need to have a guardian present."

Mabel snorted, "that's a cheap trick, the two of us are still in high school. Shouldn't that effect if we need a guardian or not?"

Shepard looked up, "the law is about age, not status when it comes to terrorizing a city."

Mabel shook her head, "we haven't been terrorizing the city, what do you think we do for fun, blow things up?"

Shepard eyed Mabel suspiciously, "no, just organize a gang."

"We are not in a gang!" Mabel corrected.

"Really?" Shepard placed her elbows on the table, "we have a source that claims you directly formed the gang with Codie Wright, and that you formed the very tech that was used in attacking the police station. What do you think you're a part of? A club or band? You and your team have caused damage, and now you will pay for it."

"What source? And what proof!?" Mabel asked.

Shepard pulled out her phone, turned it on, opened up a picture and placed it in front of Mabel. The image was of her and Will in full glowing body armor on their motorcycle. A crowd was around them cheering. Shock filled Mabel as she picked up the phone and stared at the picture. It had been taken from someone in the crowd.

Mabel shook her head, and placed the phone back on the table, "that picture isn't right…it's not what it seems."

"Really?" Shepard took the phone back and placed it in her pocket, "we have several documents about you and your gang. And every single person part of this is going down. None of you will get away."

Shepard stood up, taking the file with her.

Mabel looked at her, "we aren't a gang, and we never were…we never meant to hurt anyone or attack."

Shepard smirked, "well I guess you should look in the mirror because that's all we see."

**Sparrow Alley – 10:23 a.m.**

Codie sat in an alley. The police station was in view, but he didn't dare get closer. The dirt bike leaned against the wall, as Codie peeked around the corner. He then walked back to the dirt bike and sat behind a dumpster. Taking out a laptop from his backpack, he turned it on.

Codie started typing once it had fully loaded. He hacked into the police station and started searching through their files. It took a lot of shifting to get to the right file. He found it to be on Detective Shepard's computer, as he downloaded it from her.

Once the files were on his computer, Codie started going through them. There was a lot of speculation and not much evidence within them. Until he came across the photo, Shepard had shown Mabel.

"Now how did you get here?" he muttered to himself.

Going into detail, he found the photo to be real, and authentic. Going over it, he found other files connected to it. There were photos of the community. And it seemed that whoever had been taking them had focused on Vital Era, Vikings, and the Rooks. Mabel's, Jim's, and his team. But there was something odd when it came to his team, and something started to itch at the back of his mind.

"Okay, so the photos are on her hard drive," he clicked on a few data entries, "and the originals are stored at the state house."

Codie checked his watch, "and they are about to close, so it will take them about two days to get new ones...good."

Codie started typing furiously with a great purpose in mind. He started constructing a virus on his computer, one that would target Shepard's computer, and any police device near it. The virus took him several minutes, and a cop car passing by made him stop for a few seconds. The car didn't stop and just continued to go on its way. Shaking his head, Codie finished the last few data points on the virus and sent it to Shepard's computer the way he had collected the data in the first place.

Mabel may have been the one to build the tech for the Draconis community, but Codie had been the one to create the programs.

Codie watched as the virus went through the virtual world and landed within Shepard's computer. He turned off his laptop before putting it back into his backpack. He walked from behind the dumpster and peered around the corner, at the police station again. His nerves were on edge at being close to the people who wanted to throw him in jail, but he needed to make sure Mabel and her team got out.

**Police Station – 10:29 a.m.**

"Hey Shepard," a young officer walked up to the detective's desk, "I heard that the Mayor wants you to keep him updated, is that true?"

Shepard looked from the chair she was sitting in, "yeah, this case is a top priority because of how this gang has affected the city."

Shepard was in the main room where the detectives' desks were. The room didn't have color on its walls or floor, and a stank ruled the air causing some to have air fresheners at their desks. Shepard's desk was next to a window, so she really couldn't complain because she had a view.

"Well that's an honor, good luck," the officer walked away.

Shepard went back to looking through the papers in the file she had with her during the interviews with Jericho and Mabel. After Mabel, she had gone to Jericho, but he hadn't said anything, and there wasn't anything great on him. A random photo, but it was blurry and not the greatest of quality.

"Hey, Smith!" Shepard yelled at an officer, "you can take the two from the interrogation rooms and put them back in the holding cells."

"Okay detective," the officer in her blue uniform walked towards the interrogation rooms.

Shepard placed the file on her desk and finally looked at her computer. On the screen, she could see files being suddenly deleted.

"I need help over here!" Shepard yelled, she started typing on the computer.

A detective at the next desk looked over at her screen, "well, that's not good!"

He stood up and rushed out of the room; his goal was to find a computer specialist in the building. Shepard stared at her computer, pounding on the keyboard.

"How the heck is this happening?!" Shepard's screaming stopped the activities in the room as more officers and detectives came over to see the commotion.

The detective who had run from the room came back with a computer specialist right behind him.

"I got Traci," he panted.

Traci, the computer specialist, moved Shepard out of the way and took control of the computer. She typed faster than Shepard and moved through the computer like a wizard.

"Holy crap," Traci whispered, "who'd you tick off?"

Shepard's anger grew, "can you fix it?!"

"I'm trying, but this guy has a head start on me," Traci concentrated on the screen, "oh crap."

"What?!" Shepard asked.

"Everyone back away!" Traci ordered, "this virus can affect nearby electronics."

Everyone jumped five feet back, and the desks around Shepard were pulled away quickly. Shepard pulled out her phone and saw that the data was already gone.

"What the…!" Shepard yelled.

"Okay," Traci stopped typing, "I was able to stop it."

Shepard pushed her out of the way and looked on the screen. Most of the data had been deleted, only one blurry photo was left.

# Chapter 19

Codie peeked around the corner and looked towards the police station. The activity had increased since his virus attack. But that wasn't what he was looking at. His eyes followed a long van with the words Golden Sierra School on it. He was just barely able to see Principal Denzil driving before she parked in the police station parking lot.

Codie let out a sigh of relief and walked back to his place behind the dumpster, "I'm going to pay for that virus."

He shook his head and sat himself down by his backpack. Hanging his head, a beep from his phone caught his attention. Rubbing one of his eyes, he pulled it out and looked at the screen.

Brenton, the leader of the Soldiers team, had texted him. It read, *just heard that Vital Era is at the police station. Do we need to do anything?*

Codie ran his fingers through his curly ginger hair, as he looked at the phone with confusion. The message gave him an uneasy feeling, like the pictures from Shepard's computer, but it wasn't because of Brenton.

It was the timing of the message that had him concerned.

Shaking his head again, Codie looked at the time and stood up. He walked back over to the edge of the alley and peeked again, to look towards the police station. Waiting for a few seconds, he finally saw the Vital Era team making their way out of the station.

The five of them looked so relieved to be leaving. Shepard and Denzil came out behind the team and looked like they were having a heated conversation with each other. It was clear the virus had made Shepard angry.

Denzil shook her head and herded Mabel, Kay, Will, Baylor, and Jericho to the van in the parking lot. Shepard watched them go with an annoyed look that Codie could see from his spot.

Codie walked back to his stuff. He picked up his backpack and took the dirt bike and pushed it down the alley, away from the police station. He didn't want to ride right in front of the people looking for him.

He worked his way through the trash and garbage in the cramped area and made it to the other side of the alley, and to a street that appeared not to have police on it. He got on the bike and started it. The engine roared alive, and Codie rode down the street.

Going down the road, he kept his eyes open for any signs of people he needed to avoid.

The ride through East Waterside of Palaco City to Golden Sierra School was less stressful than the ride to the police station. Denzil drove the van, while the kids sat in the back rows. Mabel, Baylor, and Kay sat in the middle row, while Jericho and Will sat in the back of the van. They all remained quiet as the relief of leaving Shepard washed over them.

Mabel looked out a side window, and Baylor stared out the windshield. Kay leaned back in her chair and looked up at the ceiling of the vehicle. Will took out his phone, from one of his pockets, and started looking at several different messages on it. Jericho shook his head and bent over, pushing his head into the seat in front of him.

Being in the interrogation room had caused him to have a minor panic attack, but he was getting it under control now. Mabel turned to look at him, for his head pushed into her seat. She patted him on the back.

Jericho sat back up and looked into Mabel's eyes.

"Everything will be fine," she whispered to him.

He gave her a worried look, "what about the evidence?"

Mabel sighed quietly, "if it comes down to it. I want you to turn me in, so you and everyone on our team don't suffer."

Jericho shook his head, "really?"

Baylor looked over at the two of them, but he couldn't hear what they were saying because of how quiet they were being.

"Yes," Mabel put a hand on Jericho's shoulder, "they won't stop until they get justice, and if we can't fix this, someone will need to pay the price."

Jericho felt a little taken aback, "shouldn't we all pay for it then?"

Mabel gave him a sad smile, "being the team leader means taking responsibility. And that is what I will do if I need to."

Jericho shook his head again and leaned back into Mabel's seat. Mabel patted him on the back again and turned back around. Baylor gave his brother a questioning look, before grabbing one of Mabel's hands and squeezing it.

Mabel looked over at him and smiled, but she didn't say anything to him. But something inside Baylor knew that she was worried. They may have gotten out of the police station with no handcuffs on, but they felt like a collar had been placed on their necks.

Will looked up from his phone and leaned closely to Mabel, "the community knows we were in the police station."

Baylor and Mabel both looked to him.

"I thought so," Mabel nodded, "we didn't get out of there by chance."

**Golden Sierra School – 11:49 a.m.**

Denzil pulled the van into the parking lot of the school and turned off the engine, but she didn't move from her seat. She turned around and faced the kids. They all turned their attention to her. Denzil gave them each a look before talking.

"You need to tell me if any of this is true?"

Mabel frowned, "Principal Denzil, we aren't part of a gang. There's just no way we could be."

Denzil eyed Mabel, "and again tell me who that man was, who came to visit you."

Mabel shook her head, "he was a man that works for my father, I can't remember his name right now, but if you need me to get it, I can."

"Right?" Denzil sighed.

Baylor sat up straight in his seat, "is this because Jericho and Kay are dating. I know there are strict rules when it comes to stuff like that."

Kay and Jericho both gave Baylor annoyed looks, but he ignored them.

"No," Denzil turned back around to look out the windshield, "I doubt that they are even dating."

Kay perked up, "what's that supposed to mean?"

Denzil sighed again, "you know how many people have come to my office and complained about how scary you and Mabel are. I doubt anyone would want to be associated with that."

"Hey!" Kay and Mabel both said.

Jericho smiled sheepishly, "she does have a point about you two."

Kay turned to Jericho, "then why did you come over and talk to us in the first place?!"

Jericho shrugged his shoulders, "Will is a nice person. We just wanted to be nice to him. You guys just happen to come along."

Kay's jaw dropped.

Mabel snorted, "that's funny. Will is the nicest one out of the three of us."

Will blushed and hid his face in his hands.

"Okay!" Denzil abruptly said, "we are getting off the subject!"

The Vital Era team all turned their attention back to the principal in the front seat. She looked at them through the rearview mirror.

"I find it quite possible for you five to be part of something you shouldn't be," Denzil stated, "but I don't know what it could be. And if you five are in trouble, the school can help you. You just need to come forward with the info."

They all went quiet. None of them could meet Denzil's eyes. She shook her head.

"Go to class now!" she ordered.

The five of them jumped out of the van as fast as they could and ran towards the school in a hurry. Not one of them looked back, as Denzil watched them scurry away.

**Coloris Lapides – 12:13 p.m.**

Codie pushed the dirt bike through the doors of Coloris Lapides and kicked out its kickstand to place it by the scooter and trunk. He dusted off his leather jacket and shook his head. Walking around the stuff, he went to the main gym.

The sunlight had shifted, and now it danced upon the walls of the gym. Dust particles still swayed in the air, and the smell of years from the shadows rose from the ground.

Codie looked at it all. He went to the middle of the room and turned in a slow circle, so he saw the entire area. The main gym was so big that Codie and Mabel both thought a race track could be placed within it.

Looking at the area, he could almost see the track they might place around the edges of the room: a long gray metal track that circled the area, where the modified motorcycles could race along, side by side, and not needing to worry about other vehicles on the road anymore.

Codie turned his attention to another part of the gym. The bleachers were a level up and viewed the gym from a one-story height. He saw that they could place protective gear over the bleachers like a racetrack or a hockey ring. It would make the metal bleachers they had been using in the skate park look like cheap toys.

He then turned his attention to the middle of the gym. This was where he let his imagination fully work. Putting the flag and survival games in the gym would be tough work.

There would need to be a platform for the players to stand on. On this platform, they could raise obstacles, like boxes and other shapes, for the players to interact with. There would also need to be a ring around the platform like a boxing ring. Lights would be added to the floor, for they would need to keep the surrounding room dark during a game to emphasize the players in the match.

Codie smiled to himself as his mind finally saw the vision of what Mabel hoped for. It was beautiful, and he wished others could see it.

But he didn't know if it was still possible.

Codie looked down at his own hands. Seeing for a moment in his mind the work they had put into the community that was crumbling around them.

A sound from his jacket pocket interrupted his thoughts, and he sighed as his hand pulled out the phone. Opening it up, he saw a video someone had taken in secret. It showed some of the people from his community that had attacked the police station doing nefarious work.

Shock filled Codie, as he realized what they were doing to their gear in the video.

**Boys Dorm – 12:26 p.m.**

Will put his books on his bed in his room. Jericho and Baylor walked into the room, with Baylor sitting in a chair for one of the desks, and Jericho jumped onto his bed, with his face smashing into a pillow.

"Well," Baylor stretched his arms, "that was one heck of a morning, would you agree?"

Will agreed, "I was scared, I've never been in jail before."

Jericho turned over and looked at his younger friend, "with all you guys have done, you've never been to jail?"

Will shook his head, "to go to jail is to have suspicion on your team, which means you can't play in the games…but because of all the recent events, this rule doesn't mean anything anymore since everyone is a target now."

"Yay," Jericho said half-heartedly, and turn back onto his stomach.

Baylor scratched his chin, "I wonder why they released us? You said you thought it was because of the community, but is that true?"

Will nodded, "yes. There are several people in the community that have great computer skills including myself, which could have helped us get out of there. I wonder who?"

"Do you have any speculation on who?" Baylor asked.

Will shook his head. The room went quiet as the boys sat thinking to themselves about the events that had happened.

The phone in Will's pocket vibrated, and he took it out looking at the message. It was from Codie, calling for an emergency meeting later tonight.

"Weird," Will commented.

The two brothers looked at Will. They both got up and looked over his shoulder at the message on the screen.

"So…how does he expect us to go?" Jericho asked.

The other two looked to Jericho.

Jericho shrugged his shoulders, "we just got back from the police station, I doubt we will be able to leave the school for the next thirty-six months."

Baylor looked to Will, "well…what do you think?"

Will thought for a moment, "okay, so I agree we can't all go, so we should send just one of us."

The three boys looked from one to the other before saying together, "Mabel."

Will started collecting his things, "I will go tell Mabel of her new mission."

"If she can't do it, I can step in," Baylor said, "I mean, I don't mind going back to the warehouse, that is where it's going to be, right?"

"Okay I will," Will put his backpack on, "and yes that is where they will meet. That place hasn't been put on the police radar, so it is still good."

# Chapter 20

Mabel hung onto Codie as he guided the dirt bike through Palaco city. Codie had picked Mabel up from Ridder Mansion for the meeting that was going to take place tonight. She was the only one from the Vital Era team coming because it later had been decided that only leaders come.

Codie rode through the streets looking for cops or anyone who might be watching, "we're almost there."

"Okay," Mabel nodded, "how many teams are coming tonight?"

"Including the two of us, six teams will show up out of the seventeen original, that is now down to twelve teams," Codie informed her.

"So there haven't been any other teams taken down like the Vikings?" Mabel inquired.

Codie shook his head, "no, but a lot of individuals have been arrested, that's why we need to meet tonight. Those who have been fighting are filling with rage."

"Really?" Mabel thought about the rage for a moment, "and what are we going to do?"

Codie shrugged his shoulders, "to be frankly honest I don't know. That's why we are meeting. I can't make this decision on my own, and now it is a time where we must decide what we will do…after tonight, we will either be the criminals they've labeled us or maybe something more."

Mabel sighed, "I don't think we could be anything else; our community has caused so much damage."

The two of them rode through the city in silence. They went under the orange lights that illuminated the streets. Though the lights had once been mysterious, they had recently become more haunting in the last few days.

Codie guided the two of them into the warehouse selection of the city and started passing the big rectangle buildings. Mabel watched them pass by, thinking what they held within them.

They stopped in front of Warehouse sixty-two, and they got off the bike. Codie pushed it towards the door, and Mabel stood in the street looking up at the building.

The warehouse had been the start of the community. Where they had met to build the gear, to build the motorcycles, and where the games had been formed. So much had happened within its walls. And now it might see the ending.

Codie opened the door to the building and walked in with the dirt bike. The door slammed behind him. Mabel turned around and looked away from the building and to the night sky.

Letting a sigh escape from her lips, she faced the building again and walked through the door.

**Warehouse 62 – 12:58 a.m.**

Mabel walked into the dimly lit room. She saw four individuals standing in the center. Codie leaned the dirt bike against a wall and walked over with Mabel to the others. Kassidy and, Brenton were there, and the leaders of the Travelers and Storm were standing next to them. Those two team leaders looked like siblings with the same black hair and fair skin tone. The group seemed so small when considering how big they had been when starting out.

"Hey," Kassidy greeted.

"Hi," Codie answered.

Mabel nodded. Her voice felt too weak to respond to anything at the moment.

Codie nodded to the other three, "I'm glad you all could make it…I know we are having a hard time right now, but this is important."

No one responded to his words. They all had memories of troubled times in their heads, and none of them wanted to talk about it.

Codie took out his phone and sent the video he had received earlier that day to each of them. They all took out their phones and watched it.

Members from different teams were taking their gear apart and adding a weaponized laser to it. Once inside the gear, it was all put back together and tested. The beam exploded a watermelon into pieces. Then the video ended.

Emily, the leader of the Travelers, looked up from her phone, "how did you get this video?"

Codie put his phone away in a pocket, "someone anonymously sent it to me."

"How did they even figure out how to do that?" Kassidy shook her head.

"That's the same question I was thinking," Seth, leader of the Storm, put in, "I know at the start of the construction of the Draconis games we did have lasers like that, but not many people knew...I pretty sure all those who fight against the cops didn't know about it."

"Well, Abbie from the Arch of the Lily team did know about the laser. She wasn't directly involved, only Rooks and Magic were involved in it," Brenton pointed out.

"That's true," Kassidy confirmed, "my team did their best with the gear, but none of them told anyone else."

Codie rubbed his hands together, "my team said they wouldn't tell anyone about it, but maybe someone else might have gotten close, or it could be someone not part of our teams anymore."

Everyone looked at Codie.

"What do you mean? Has someone from your team gone rogue?" Abbie asked.

Codie looked around the big empty room, "I don't think we should focus on that right now, but let's go into the backroom. This place is too open for this conversation."

He walked towards the room, and everyone followed.

**Backroom – 1:15 a.m.**

The six of them walked into the room, Kassidy turned on the light.

"So you know who the rat is?" Brenton asked.

Codie sighed, "I believe I know, but right now there aren't any facts."

"Well, who do you think it is?" Seth inquired.

Codie shook his head, "I don't want to say any names right now, for I could be completely wrong…what we need to talk about is the next attack that will happen."

"You think another attack is going to happen?" Abbie asked.

Kassidy snorted, "why do you think they are putting those lasers in their gear? It isn't for show."

"I agree with Kassidy, those lasers are being put in for a reason," Mabel chimed in.

"Okay," Abbie agreed, "but what do you expect us to do exactly. It's not like we have those lasers in our gear. We can't do anything."

"That's why we are all here," Codie explained, "we are the last teams in our community that haven't lost our minds. We need to decide. Are we going to let this happen or will we stop it before anyone else gets hurt? We went away from the lasers because of how much damage they would cause."

"We should stop it," Mabel stated.

Brenton snorted, "then we will be turning ourselves into the police. The reason some of us haven't joined the other side is that we have families we need to take care of. None of us want to go to jail."

The room went silent.

Codie looked at everyone before speaking, "we are part of this community, just like those who attacked the police. We may not be holding the gun, but we will be pulled down with those who are. You may not want to go to jail, but if you do nothing. You might just set yourself up for the steel bars anyway."

"You don't know that," Seth pointed out, "and personally I don't think we need to do anything. I doubt they will hurt anyone; they're probably doing it to intimidate people."

"I wouldn't believe that," Mabel spoke up, "and if you don't feel the need to fight, fine…but I know I helped cause this, by building those motorcycles and the gear. I may not want to go to jail, but I'm not going to let someone else gets hurt just because I'm too selfish to face my consequences."

Mabel shook her head and walked out of the backroom. Everyone watched her leave, but no one followed her. She went to the dirt bike and walked it out of the warehouse.  She started it up and started riding away from the building.

**Coloris Lapides – 2:02 a.m.**

Codie got out of Kassidy's car and walked into Coloris Lapides. The building was dark inside, and he hit his knee against an object.

"Ow," he limped away from the object.

"Codie?" Mabel whispered in the darkness.

"Ah!" Codie yelled.

Mabel turned on her phone's flashlight and gave him a funny look. Codie blinked his eyes and settled down.  Mabel sat on her team's trunk.

"You okay?" Mabel asked him.

Codie sighed, "I'm fine.  I have a lantern if you want me to turn it on?"

"Sounds good."

Codie walked over to his backpack and pulled out an old electric camping lantern.  He turned it on, and the light illuminated a small area around them.  He placed it on the trunk next to Mabel.

"Should you be getting back to school?" Codie asked her, as he sat down next to her.

"I want to talk to you," Mabel explained.

Codie gave Mabel his attention, "okay, I'm listening."

Mabel took in a deep breath, "I'm going to fight against the attack. I may not know when it is, but I'm going to try…This has gone on for too long, and I'm tired of being viewed as a gang member. Either I do something to prove we aren't a gang, or I turn myself in for the terrorizing I've been a part of."

Codie rubbed his chin, "okay…I will help you, but what about your team. Are they going to fight along with you?"

Mabel let out a breath of air softly, "I was hoping they wouldn't need to get involved."

Codie sighed, "Mabel, even if the teams we met with tonight had all their teammates to fight on our side, we would still need your team, just to try and make a difference."

Mabel agreed, "I understand that, but I feel that if they don't want to. They don't have to."

"So you are going to tell them?" Codie gave Mabel a questioning look.

"Yes," Mabel looked at her hands, "I did consider not telling them, but I'm not good at lying when it comes to my teammates…I will see if they will join this fight, that will end the games."

Codie looked up at the dark ceiling, "it may end the way we do things now, but Mabel we still might be able to save some parts of it…We can make this work."

Mabel smiled a sad smile and stood up from the trunk, "I'm going back to school now. I will tell you what my teammates' responses will be."

Codie smiled at her, "don't worry. I already know what they will say to you."

Mabel frowned at him, before pushing the dirt bike back out of the building.

**Ridder Mansion – 2:59 a.m.**

The night sky blanketed the whole city. The lights shined brightly on it but only caused it to become more romantic. If the city didn't have the chaos bubbling within, some people might think it was a nice place to live.

But trouble was tearing it at the seams. Some people didn't feel the trouble, but many were worried. Would their city fall? No one knew the answer.

Mabel rode onto Ridder Mansion driveway and got off the bike. She pushed it behind one of the walls. The night air coolly wrapped itself around Mabel, and she breathed it in deeply. Mabel walked away from the bike and towards the Ridder Mansion. She walked up to the building and stared at the crumbling house. Pieces of the roof were on the ground, and several parts of the wall had fallen within. She could get into the building if there was a desire to see the inside.

Only the sounds of the night greeted her; there wasn't anything else to welcome her. She couldn't see any stars, and there didn't seem to be any moon out tonight. It was only the light from the streetlights; even the Golden Sierra School was dark except for emergency lights that always stayed on. The orange light formed its pools of light on the street, casting an eerie glow upon the old mansion.

This mansion must have been beautiful when it was first built. Probably the biggest building in its day. Must have made every neighbor jealous of its grandeur. Mabel wondered how something so great could deteriorate to something unrecognizable, and what the original builders would think of it now.

"I wonder what it would be like to see this mansion when its windows weren't broken and the paint wasn't faded," Mabel whispered to herself.

Sighing Mabel turned back to Golden Sierra School. One of the newest buildings she had seen, and one of the dullest buildings she had ever known, but it had become home after so many years of living there.

"Will we be forgotten like Ridder Mansion?" Mabel mumbled thoughts of her team and the community whirled around in her head.

If she could, Mabel would try and save the people she had worked with for the past few years. But most people couldn't see their rage, and there wasn't any way to stop it. They would need to crash, and Mabel was finally willing to block them.

She walked away from the building and back to the street. Mabel made her way back to the dullest building she had ever known. She went back to school. There was a thought in the back of her mind that it might be her the last time in the school.

# Chapter 21

The Vital Era team walked down one of the hallways in Golden Sierra School. They all had on their navy blue uniforms. The five of them blended into the sea of students, and could almost be lost to the waves of kids trying to get to their next class.

Kay and Jericho talked with each other in front of the others, as they all walked down the hall. They smiled at each other. Kay had helped Jericho overcome the panic attack that had happened at the police station.

Will and Baylor talked with each other; they discussed school assignments that needed to get done. A big project concerning an English paper was coming up, and the two of them didn't know where to start.

Mabel walked to Will's side. She listened for a little bit to her friends' conversation. But her thoughts kept pulling her away. She hadn't told them about the video from Codie, or the meeting that happened last night. They had asked, but she had told them they would need to wait until lunchtime.

She knew Codie would have wanted her to tell them right away, but giving this information to them might destroy their last hope for the community. Time was ticking, and she knew that the Vital Era team needed to know what was happening.

Sighing to herself Mabel looked over at her brother and friend, they were deep in their conversation about which book to study for the English paper.

"Hey," she said to them.

They stopped their conversation and turned their attention to her.

"Yeah?" Will asked.

"So I was thinking about what happened last night," she started.

The speaker system in the school came to life, causing everyone who could hear it to cringe at the sudden squeaking.

"Students, please listen quickly," the voice said over the system.

Everyone stopped talking, including Mabel and her friends.

"We need these students to come to the office immediately, Mabella Overton, Wilt Overton, Kayleigh Eldred, Baylor Alan, and Jericho Alan. The rest of you get to class before the second bell rings," the speaker system turned off with more squeaking before leaving the hallways in the school silent.

Everyone waited a few seconds before continuing their conversations.

"Well that can't be good," Kay looked back to Mabel.

Mabel shrugged her shoulders, "we can't run, might as well see if we are going to jail again."

Jericho looked at his hands, as his nerves became tense. Kay shook her head, before putting her arm around Jericho's shoulders and comforting him. He smiled at her as the team started their long walk to the office.

**Front Office – 10:30 a.m.**

The five of them walked into the office, and Mrs. Stevenson directed them to the five chairs outside of Denzil's office. The office was empty. Mrs. Stevenson typed furiously at her keyboard and didn't give the students another look, as she went back to work.

Jericho looked back at his hands and rubbed them together. Kay still had an arm on his shoulders, and now she reached her free hand and grabbed one of his hands.

"Hey Jericho, don't worry about this," Kay whispered to him, "Mabel has it all figured out. We aren't going back to jail…there's no need to worry."

Jericho gave Kay a worried look before looking to Mabel. Jericho and Mabel stared at each other, as the memory of her telling him to turn her in came to their minds. Jericho knew if he turned Mabel in that the others would view him as the rat, and that made him more worried than going to jail.

Mabel leaned over Will to talk to Kay, "Kay, we need to talk about my backup plan. It's not what it seems."

All the members of the Vital Era team gave her a weird look.

"What do you mean?" Will asked, "you do have a plan, right?"

"I do, but it's a last resort plan," Mabel started to explain.

"Last resort," Baylor shook his head, "those are like when ships explode, or people run into a burning building to never come out again."

"Well…" Jericho tilted his head a little.

Kay, Baylor, and Will looked from Jericho to Mabel before settling back on Jericho.

"Exactly what is the backup plan?" Kay stared into Jericho's eyes.

"I think Mabel should explain it; she's just so better at it," Jericho gave a nervous smile, "and she came up with it too."

They all turned their attention back to Mabel. She gave them an awkward smile.

"Well…" she started with a nervous chuckle.

But before she could finish her sentence, Denzil and Shepard walked into the room. Denzil was in her gray dress suit, and Shepard was wearing a black pantsuit. The two of them together looked like lawyers going into the courtroom.

"This is ridiculous!" Denzil stated, "you can't come here every day to harass my students!"

"Do I need to have the Mayor call you again?!" Shepard stepped into Denzil's personal space, "this is about security for the city!"

Vital Era gazed up at the two adults in wonder. They did remind them of lawyers battling each other. Denzil looked at the students, straightened her suit, and pointed to her office.

"Detective Shepard would like to have a minute of your time in my office," Denzil directed.

They got up from their chairs and walked in.

**Denzil's Office – 10:39 a.m.**

Baylor, Mabel, Will, Kay, and Jericho sat in the chairs in front of Denzil's desk and waited as Shepard sat behind it with Denzil giving her a nasty look. Shepard ignored the look and pulled out her phone from her pocket and turned it on. She flipped through a few pictures before settling on one and placing it on the table.

The image was a teammate of the Seals team being put onto the ground as handcuffs were put around his wrist. His helmet had come off somehow, and they could see blood coming from a cut on his cheek.

"His name is Alec," Shepard watched their reactions, "but you all already knew that."

Baylor sat up straight, "I didn't know his name. I'm not even sure I've seen this man before. But then again I have seen a lot of people, so maybe I have seen him."

Shepard gave him an annoyed look, but he looked at the others and shrugged his shoulders. He was honest. He hadn't met Alec before.

Mabel rubbed her chin, "I know a Alex, but not one Alec. That name isn't as popular as it used to be."

"That was popular once?" Kay asked.

Shepard let an angry sigh out before changing the picture on the phone. The image showed a wounded police officer. Blood came from her side, and it appeared she had passed out, while others were trying to help her. The image unsettled the kids. Shepard continued to flip through the photos. Each one had someone hurt, from members of the games to police officers.

After going through seventeen photos, Shepard leaned back in the chair, "this was the attack that happened to the police station. We're lucky no one died during that attack, but several were hospitalized."

No one was joking now. The entire Vital Era team had gone quiet and solemn. Mabel's heart started to beat faster in her chest, as old memories came into her mind.

Before Christmas last year, a crash had happened. Mabel was behind the impact. A member of the Knights team had been riding their motorcycle when a truck driver fell asleep at the wheel. The young man had been Gary Newman. A very nice young man. He died on the street, with his blood dripping into the gutter.

Those images came back to Mabel, and fear followed after them.

"You know," Shepard shook her head, "even with all the arrests we have, none of them have talked to us. I would like to know how such loyalty can be put into your gang members."

Denzil became furious at Shepard, "how dare you to show such images to my students, that's enough of your harassment. I want you out of my school!"

Shepard stood up, "when you five are ready to talk, please contact me."

Shepard put a card on the table and walked out of the room with Denzil escorting her.

**Girls' Dorm – 10:54 a.m.**

Mabel walked along the girls' dorm hallway alone. Only a few girls rushed from the hallway to get to class. Mabel hung her head and made her way to her room. Opening the door, she walked in, and slowly closed it behind her.

Walking slowly to her bed, Mabel softly laid on it and curled into a ball. Tears streamed down her face, as she finally let herself cry. She didn't make any noise as her body shook with sorrow and fear.

She could see Gary, she could see the truck, she could see the crash.

She remembered riding her motorcycle behind Gary. It had only been riders for that game, and that was the only good thing. They had been both going down a big street in Midtown when suddenly a guy, driving a huge truck, barreled through a red light. He had fallen asleep at the wheel. His truck slammed into Gary and smashed into a building along the side of the road.

Mabel had stopped her bike in shock. Gary's bike and been smashed into oblivion, but he had been thrown from the crash after the first impact.

He had landed on the sidewalk. His body half in the street. Mabel, in her shock, walked to him.

Gary had still been alive when she got to him. A piece of metal had pierced his back, puncturing a lung and a main artery. But she didn't know that till after. Even with the blood that poured out of his back, her shock didn't let her mind move to understand what was happening.

Mabel had taken off Gary's helmet. He coughed blood after it was removed, and blood dripped from the helmet as Mabel placed it on the ground.

Mabel's tears increased as her mind remembered the last part of the memory. The last words Gary had said.

"Please tell Hal to give it to her," he had said with his last full breath.

After that Mabel remembered very little. They had told her that Hal, the leader of the Knight team, the team Gary had been on, had rushed over with Codie, Joi, and Kassidy because the camera in Mabel's helmet had been showing the scene going on. They got there before the police but had to leave Gary's body.

Mabel shook her head and made her body curl up more on the bed, as the memory finished its course.

"I wish," she cried to herself, "I could have changed it, I wish I could have stopped it…I wish none of it had happened."

Her eyes stop producing tears, and Mabel calmed down. After several minutes of silence, the coming terror came to her. The next attack, whenever it might be, would be worse than Gary's death.

**Lunchroom – 12:06 p.m.**

Will, Jericho, Baylor, and Kay sat at a lunchroom table quietly eating their food. They didn't pick at it or complain, they just ate it. Mabel walked up to the table and sat down. She didn't have any food, for her appetite was gone.

Her team all sat on the other side of the table and looked like a council she had to please. Her eyes were swollen, but that was the only sign of her tears.

"We need to talk," she said to them.

They all looked at her, quietly waiting for the news that was to come.

"Last night Codie shared a video…It showed the teams that attacked the police station putting weaponized lasers into their gear…Their next attack will have casualties," Mabel informed them.

"I can't believe we have come down to this," Kay whispered to herself.

"They can't be serious?!" Baylor asked.

"Why aren't they stopping? Are they really going to attack?" Will shook his head, he looked like he was about to cry.

Jericho remained silent and stared at his hands.

"I've realized, that it's my duty to stop them," Mabel watched the four of them carefully, "I'm not asking you to follow me into this battle."

"Why do you have to fight?" Will asked with the innocence of a child.

"Will, this is our fault. We let this build up, we let it form, and now we've let it get out of control. We may have never been a gang, but we are a terrorist organization now. With the attack on the police station, our innocences is gone. And because of my part, it is my responsibility to fix it. I'm not going to let people get hurt anymore. I'm going to tear down our community and stop it if I can...I'm going to confess to everything," Mabel finished her statement.

"Why would you confess?" Kay slammed her fists on the table.

"I'm taking responsibility, and I'm tired of hiding," Mabel answered, "I want you all to understand, that I don't want any of you to turn yourselves in."

"What about our responsibility?" Baylor asked.

"I pulled you into this, I pulled you all into this," Mabel stood up from the table, "I hope I'm clear on this."

No one said anything.

Mabel nodded, "I also want you to know that if you choose to fight with me, it is very likely you will get hurt. This isn't a game; it's a war."

Kay looked up at her friend, "do you want us to fight?"

"I wish I didn't have to ask you," Mabel answered.

She turned away from her friends and walked out of the lunchroom.

# Chapter 22

Mabel walked briskly to Ridder Mansion. She didn't care if other students, or if teachers saw her. Being secretive was finally too much for her, and now she simply didn't care about breaking the rules of the school. Mabel was still in her navy blue uniform, but that didn't stop her from going across the street and up the driveway of Ridder Mansion.

Kay, Baylor, Will, and Jericho ran after her. They were nervous about being in their school uniforms in the middle of the day, crossing a street that they shouldn't be on, but they were more worried about their friend.

"Mabel wait," Kay called out, "can't we wait a minute."

Mabel didn't stop and walked behind the wall. The group followed her behind the wall and watched as she uncovered the dirt bike.

"What are you going to do?" Baylor asked.

"I'm going to our gym and am going to prepare for the attack. I'm not letting the police station fall," Mabel informed them.

"But we're just kids," Jericho pointed out.

Mabel stood up and gave the group a serious look, "our actions have nothing to do with our age. These are serious crimes that have been and will be committed. We may be kids, but that doesn't change anything."

Jericho looked back at the school and saw that nothing had changed. Everything looked normal. He wished they could go back.

"What do you want us to do?" Will asked.

Mabel sighed, "as I said before. I'm going to war, I wish I didn't have to ask you, but will you help me?"

The question hung in the air. Even Baylor and Kay went silent. Fighting violence wasn't something they were prepared for. They weren't the police force; they didn't have any training. Mabel took their silence as an answer, she pulled out the bike and started pushing it down the driveway. She felt like crying again, but held it back. Baylor shook his head and hurried after her.

Putting a hand on her shoulder, he stopped her, "Mabel, I'll help you. I agree with what you said, and am willing to help with this"

Mabel smiled at him, as relief flooded her.

"Yeah, and you aren't going without me," Kay turned around and faced them, "what do you want us to do?"

Jericho gave Kay a weird look, "us?"

Kay smirked at him, "you know the two of you were going to come with us, there's no way you two are not joining this adventure."

"It could be our last," Will pointed out.

"Then we enjoy it," Kay said, "what do we need to do?"

Mabel smiled, "the three of you go and collect a change of clothes, I not sure we will be coming back to school. Baylor and I will go to the gym, then to the junkyard to collect items. You three need to figure out a way to get to the gym by yourselves."

Kay agreed, "we will do that."

Kay took Will and Jericho by the arms and led them back to the school. Baylor sat on the bike and waited for Mabel.

**Petal Junkyard – 1:14 p.m.**

Baylor stopped the dirt bike while Mabel hung onto him. They got off the bike and viewed the junkyard from within. Petal Junkyard had been abandoned by the community; there hadn't been anyone there except the people who worked there. Those individuals had been on the payroll to keep quiet about everything happening inside.

The containers were still there, but they all were empty now. Nothing but garbage. And that was what Mabel wanted.

"Okay, we need to look for any mechanical parts, or even metal parts," Mabel pointed to a section of the garbage.

"Sounds good," Baylor walked over to the pile and started digging around.

Mabel quickly walked around the area, looking into every container there making sure nothing could be salvaged from them. She finished her track around the junkyard and went back to Baylor to help dig through the trash. He had already collected a pile of forgotten metal pieces from an old computer.

"That's a good pile," Mabel complimented.

"Thanks," Baylor stared into the trash, "I was shocked by Codie's reaction to you."

Mabel concurred, "I know. Sometimes he's just full of surprises."

Baylor stopped working in the trash and looked at Mabel. She stopped too and returned the look.

"I don't mean I don't get it. I understand that he doesn't want you to drop out of school. I was shocked by how passionate he was about your future," Baylor explained.

"We aren't dating, if that's what you're asking," Mabel felt a little awkward with the conversation.

Baylor shook his head, "I know you two aren't dating. But your friendship is just so strong; I've never seen one like it."

Mabel shrugged her shoulders, "well we've been through a lot. I honestly don't know what else to tell you. Codie is a caring person; I'm not the only one he treats like this. He treats his team like that, and Kassidy's team. We were the ones that formed the community."

Baylor nodded and bent back over the trash, "okay. I get it."

Mabel shrugged her shoulders again and went back to the trash as well. They scavenged through it in silence for a few moments. After taking out an old broken computer, pieces of a bicycle, and the ice maker part of a fridge. They started packing the items into a bag they had brought with them.

"Will this be enough?" Baylor asked.

"No, but it will be a good start, the computer will help us with our gear. And the bicycle parts with our motorcycles, but Codie asked for pieces of a fridge, I don't know what they will be used for," Mabel explained.

"Well, let's get our treasure home then," Baylor got on the bike.

Mabel held on to the bag and got on behind Baylor, the two of them rode out of the junkyard.

**Coloris Lapides – 1:46 p.m.**

Baylor pushed the dirt bike into the front area of Coloris Lapides. Mabel carried the bag of items in, and the two of them looked around the area. Noises were coming from the main gym, and they walked over to the door. Opening it up, they saw Codie and Kay talking about a piece of gear, while Will and Jericho were setting up the area.

They walked over to the group, and Mabel put the bag of items on a table.

Codie looked over at them, "what did you find?"

"Computer and bicycle parts, and a piece of a fridge," Mabel informed him.

"Good," Codie walked over to the bag and started digging through it.

Codie's leather jacket was off, and all he had on was a t-shirt and jeans. Kay, Will, and Jericho all changed into their street clothes, leaving Baylor and Mabel as the only ones in the school uniforms.

Kay threw each of them a bag, "here are some clothes."

"Thanks," Mabel walked towards the bathroom.

Baylor looked in his bag, "you didn't pack my clothes, right?"

Kay smirked at him, "no, your brother did."

"Oh, good, then there will be clothes in here," Baylor smiled and ran off to the bathroom before Kay could throw anything at him.

"You twit!" Kay yelled at him.

Kay turned her attention back to Codie; he was still going through the bag of parts that had been brought. She walked up to him and watched as the items were sorted out.

"Why fridge parts?" Kay asked.

"I need to build a special tool, and fridge parts have some of the things I need for its construction of the tool," Codie explained.

Kay tilted her head, she picked up a bicycle part and started examining it, "have any of the other teams decided to join us?"

"No," Codie sighed, but continued to sort, "it's just you guys and some of my team."

Kay gave Codie a weird look, "some of your team, who's not helping?"

Codie shook his head, "it's not like that, and right now isn't the time to talk about it."

"What?" Kay found Codie's response to be unbelievable.

"I think we should take the motorcycles to the warehouse," Codie called over to the other boys, stopping the conversation with Kay, "I'm collecting fridge parts for a tool to help set up a new network system for our bikes and gear. That's going to be noisy, better to do it at the warehouse."

Mabel and Baylor came back from the bathroom as Codie announced the next step in their plan.

"Okay," Mabel agreed, "but we're going to need more parts, how about Jericho, Will, and Baylor go to a different junkyard to get more, while we take the motorcycles to the warehouse?"

"Sounds good," Codie took out keys from his pocket, "I have a truck that can take one motorcycle at a time, so the cops don't pull us over."

**Coyote Junkyard – 2:34 p.m.**

Jericho tripped over a black bag and smacked into his brother, Baylor lost his balance and fell over. They landed on dirt, and the two of them yelped at the sudden descent to the ground. Will watched the whole thing from a few feet away, and looked at his two friends on the ground.

"You two okay?" he asked.

"Peachy," Baylor mumbled, he pushed his brother off, who sat up from the dirt and shook his head.

"Sorry Baylor," Jericho apologized, "I didn't see that bag."

"It's okay," Baylor stood up and helped his brother stand, the two of them brushed their clothes off.

Will went back to digging through the trash, as did his two friends. They had found two fridges, and they were taking them apart. But there was still much more to be found in the junkyard. The Coyote Junkyard had always been a great source of materials, but the reason it hadn't been used for the community's place was that it was too close to the other parts of Palaco City.

Will worked on the freezer part of a fridge, while Baylor and Jericho were taking apart the door of the other fridge. That was why they didn't notice Kassidy walking up to them from the dirt path in the junkyard. She watched them work for a little bit; she didn't understand what they were doing.

"So, this is new," she commented.

The boys all jumped and turned around quickly, their hearts pounding with surprise.

"Kassidy! What are you doing here?!" Baylor asked.

"Well, I've been looking for you guys and Codie, but you're all so hard to find," Kassidy smiled at them.

"Why are you looking for us?" Will asked.

"Well, we've decided to fight," Kassidy informed them.

"Do you mean your team?" Jericho asked.

Kassidy shook her head, "nope, the four teams that haven't fought at all, have all agreed to fight with you guys."

The boys shared a look between the three of them, before turning back to Kassidy. She waited patiently for their response.

Will jumped away from the fridge and hugged Kassidy, "that's such great news."

Kassidy smiled at him; he released her.

"So what do you need help with?" she asked them.

"Well, we need to get parts for gear and motorcycles, since there's a lot more of us now," Jericho started directing.

Kassidy whistled loudly. Her team and the other three teams came walking into the junkyard. They all started collecting from the trash around the area.

"Now why were you taking the fridges apart?" she asked them.

Baylor shrugged his shoulders, "Codie needs them."

**Warehouse 62 – 3:51 p.m.**

The usually empty warehouse had two modified motorcycles and several tables with tools and gear on it. Mabel was working on a helmet, while Kay and Codie were working on one of the modified motorcycles.

"Okay, I got the wire, can you connect the tube?" Kay asked Codie.

He worked with a tube and clicked it into a section of the motor, "there, I got it."

The two of them stepped back and admired their work for a second. A knock at the door caught their attention.

"I'll get it," Kay sighed, she walked over to the door and opened it.

Kassidy was standing in the doorway, "hey Kay, how's life?"

Mabel and Codie looked at the door and saw Kassidy, Jericho, Will, Baylor, and the rest of the teams standing behind them.

Kay tilted her head, "are we hosting a party?"

"Ha," Kassidy walked in with the rest of the group following behind, they all had bags of parts.

"They've decided to join us," Will ran to Mabel to tell her the good news.

Mabel smiled at her little brother, "that's great."

Kassidy walked over to Codie and shook his hand, "what can we do to help?"

"It's great to see you," Codie smiled, "could you bring the motorcycles in, we need to update them. We're working on a new network for our gear."

"Why a new network?" Kassidy asked.

Codie continued to smile, "we need to be on a separate network so they can't see our movements by tracking the network we share now."

The teams started socializing with Mabel and Kay, and everyone started taking up stations to work on gear, while others left to get their stuff. But Kassidy stayed with Codie.

"So, you're going to build the new network?" Kassidy asked.

Codie nodded.

"How long will it take?"

Codie rubbed the back of his neck, "I started work on it after the first attack on the police station."

"Wow," Kassidy shook her head, "you were planning this for that long?"

Kassidy and Codie looked at the group of people working. Everyone was doing something.

Kassidy scrunched up her nose, "I don't see your team, where are they?"

Codie became serious, "they are working on a different part of the plan. Don't worry they will be with us when we take up our position to defend the police station…is that Garnett, I thought he got arrested?"

Kassidy flinched at his words, "he did, but since we are coming into the light anyway, I thought he could come back."

Kassidy watched Codie for any disagreement, but he agreed with her.

"Sounds good to me, we need all the help we can get," he said.

# Chapter 23

**Palaco City, October 13, 2090 – 8:03 a.m.**

The time had arrived and was confirmed by more than one source, that the attack was going to happen soon on the Police Station. The plan that they had been working on for days now was finally being put into action. Codie was going ahead of the teams, to try and keep the police in the station.

Two semi-trucks carried two old containers from the junkyard. The part of the community that had not taken part in the fight were inside the two containers. Inside the first container were the Vital Era, Magic, and Soldiers teams. In the other container were the Rooks, Travelers, and Storm teams.

Mabel was in the first container; it was mostly dark except for the glowing armored suits everyone was wearing and motorcycle lights. The group had agreed to let their lights be yellow, because that was a color rarely used by other teams, and it would make easier to see teammates. Everyone had their full armor on, including their helmets. Mabel sat on her team's motorcycle, with Kay and Jericho on the back of it.

Kay and Jericho both had their gear on, with their bracelets glowing brown on their wrist and ankles. They were prepared for battle.

"How do you think Will and Baylor are holding up?" Kay asked through the helmet's communication system.

Their communication system was set up, so it was only connected to the three of them.

"I bet they're doing just fine," Mabel said comfortingly.

"Really? I don't understand why they have to be on the container's roof while we're driving," Jericho complained.

"Jericho," Mabel turned so she could look at his helmet, "once we reach the field, I'm pretty sure there won't be any free time for any of us. One of the sources called into Kassidy and informed her they were on the move already and that we need to hurry over to the station."

"Don't worry," Kay chimed in, "those two are tough and will have each other's back, and Kassidy is driving, so she'll keep them safe while she's in charge."

"That doesn't calm my stomach," Jericho mumbled.

Kay turned so she could stare at Jericho's helmet now, "don't you worry about anything. Codie's plan is going to work. He thinks out every possible thing; he's the great mastermind of our community."

The container lunged forward with the speed of the semi-truck increasing. This made everyone in the container nervous as the battlefield was coming closer.

"Well, we can't turn back," Mabel whispered, she faced the front of her motorcycle and looked at the metal doors that held them inside.

A red light went on in all the helmets, signifying their approach to the police station.

**Police Station – 8:11 a.m.**

Codie had on his leather jacket, and his curly ginger hair had been pulled back so it wouldn't be in his face. He looked up at the police station and sighed a little. Shaking his head, he walked into the building without a second thought. There was a desk at the front, with a secretary sitting there. She looked up and greeted him.

But Codie just walked past her and went towards the main room of the station where the detective desks were. He looked around the area, with very few people even noticing him, despite his ranking as one of the most wanted criminals at the moment. His eyes landed on Detective Shepard. She was wearing a white collared shirt with dress pants at the moment.

Codie walked across the room and up to Shepard's desk. He stood by it as she typed on her keyboard.

"What do you want?" she asked without looking up from her computer screen.

"I want to report a crime about to happen," Codie informed her.

She sighed dramatically, "go to the front desk, and the secretary will direct you to the right officer."

"She'll just direct me to you," he pointed out.

Shepard shook her head, "really?!"

She finally turned her attention to him, and shocked filled her as she recognized his face, "your Codie Wright!"

Shepard stood up from her desk and pointed a finger at him. Codie gave the detective a funny look, at her sudden reaction.

"Well I just go by Codie," he smiled at her, "I would like to report a crime about to happen. That I think you and this police station should be worried about."

"And what crime is that?" Shepard put her hands on her hips, "are you going to rob a store?"

Codie shook his head, "no, I'm not the one going to commit the crime, I just know it's going to happen."

Shepard opened a drawer from her desk and pulled out handcuffs, "and what's going to happen?"

Codie was turned around by Shepard as she placed the handcuffs on his wrist. He didn't resist.

"The police station is going to be attacked again," he informed her.

"What do you mean?" Shepard turned him back around.

"The people who attacked you before are coming back, and this time they are coming for blood," Codie gave her a small smile, "but don't worry. I have my friends coming to help out with this problem."

Shepard shook her head again and looked around the room, "Smith! Come take this man and put him in a holding cell!"

An officer in a blue uniform came running up to them and grabbed Codie by the arm. Codie was led out of the room, as Shepard picked up a phone. She started making calls.

**Sparrow Street – 8:24 a.m.**

Kassidy drove, in her full armor, the first semi-truck with Vital Era, Soldiers and her team inside. She came up the street and could see the police station. The front was empty of people, and relief flooded her as she saw that. But her relief didn't last long, as from down the street that was directly in front of the station she could see modified motorcycles and armored people coming.

"Crap," Kassidy smacked a button on her arm, it caused a blue light to turn on within all the helmets, "here we go."

Kassidy drove the semi-truck right up to the police station doors, smashing into part of the building. The impact shook the building and stopped the truck. The windshield was cracked, but there hadn't been anyone hurt in the sudden stop. Kassidy looked out the passenger window and saw the bikes coming closer, but they weren't coming towards the police station unhindered now.

Baylor and Will stood up from the top of the container on the semi-truck, they each had their gear on. Will's bracelets were glowing red, and he was firing his red light fire at the coming motorcycles. Baylor had his metal water pouches glowing blue with his gloves. He started firing as well.

The other semi-truck pulled in front of the first one and stopped without crashing into anything. Two other armored people were on top of that container, and they jumped off the container to the back. They opened it up, and the motorcycles started coming out from within. They ran to the other container and opened it up. All the bikes were released.

The yellow motorcycles started riding against the other side. Kassidy could hear people yelling inside the police station, as they realized the front door couldn't be opened anymore.

Kassidy opened the passenger door and crawled out of the smashed vehicle; she climbed to the top of her container. Her armor scraped against the container, and her cauldron strapped to her hip banged against the side. Getting on top of it, Kassidy walked over to the boys and turned on her cauldron. The inside of the small black cauldron glowed bright yellow, and with special gloves on Kassidy reached inside and pulled out a bottle made of light filled with yellow particles. She threw the bottle and started helping the others with the battle.

Everyone on Codie's side of the community didn't have to worry about hitting one of their teammates in the field. This was the reason they constructed a new network for their systems. The other side could still knock out their power, but that side could also knock out their teammates.

**Penguin Street – 8:41 a.m.**

Mabel passed between two opposing bikes, while Kay and Jericho flung brown light rocks towards them. They missed the bikes, but one of the passengers was hit turning the armor off. Mabel dodged an attack aimed at them and skidded the bike to a stop.

The whole street was full of glowing motorcycles and armored people, very few individuals armor had been powered down. It seemed that some of the fighters had fallen off of their bikes and were turning into fists instead of gear.

"Ready!?" Mabel asked into the helmets system.

Not waiting for an answer from Kay or Jericho, Mabel turned the bike to go back into the chaos.

"I haven't seen any use of that special laser," Kay pointed out.

"I don't think they are using it on us," Jericho guessed.

Mabel tensed up as her eye caught sight of a motorcycle charging at them from her side mirrors. She sped her bike up and jumped onto the sidewalk, the bike followed. Jericho and Kay couldn't get a good angle on it, as it continued to shift from their view. The motorcycle didn't have any passenger on it, just a rider, and the rider was preparing the two hooks on the bike.

The hooks were fired, one of them missed, but the other missed Jericho and hit Kay in the back of her armor latching onto her. Jericho saw the hook and tried to pull it out.

"What hit me?!" Kay tried to see what was in her back, but couldn't.

"A hook!" Jericho answered he tried to remove it.

"Get it out!" Mabel ordered.

Before Jericho could wiggle it anymore, the bike behind them reeled in the line. It took Kay off their bike, along with Jericho who forgot to let go when being pulled. The two of them slammed into the pavement below and tumbled behind the bike they were connected to until they were being dragged behind on the sidewalk. Mabel saw her two teammates behind her through her side mirrors.

"Crap, hang on!" Mabel jumped off the sidewalk and started going towards the two semi-trucks.

"What do you expect us to do?!" Jericho's panic voice yelled into the communications.

Kay and Jericho's armor scraped against the ground as they shifted from sidewalk to asphalt, Kay was being pulled from her back, her front was being dragged on the asphalt while Jericho hung onto the line connected to the hook scraping his back against the ground.    Mabel led

the bike in front of the containers on the trucks, and without the other rider

realizing it.  Baylor and Will fired at the bike.

The charging bike was struck by red and blue lights from the top of

the container and powered down.  Kay and Jericho rushed past the bike as it

stopped.  They were yanked at the end of the hook, and Kay came loose

with Jericho still hanging onto the line as she was flung a few yards away.

**Penguin and Sparrow Intersection – 9:03 a.m.**

"You two okay?!" Mabel asked, she stopped her bike and turned in

her seat to see her teammates.

"Yeah," Kay stood up from the asphalt and walked over to Jericho,

who still hung on to the line.

Kay's armor was damaged, but the hook hadn't touched her, so there

wasn't any wound.  Mabel sighed with relief at seeing her friend okay.

A strange sound from the chaos in the street made her look away

from her friends and at an armored individual aiming a light firing rifle at

her.  A strange blue beam was building up inside the barrel of the gun.  The

blue beam fired, and it struck Mabel's bike.  It struck her front wheel

causing it to explode with parts going everywhere.  The small explosion sent Mabel and her motorcycle flying backward. She landed hard on the ground with the bike landing on top of her, pinning her down.

"Mabel!" Kay cried.

Jericho and Kay ran over to their friend, while Will, Baylor, and the other three members on the container's top started firing at the rifle wielder. The rifle wielder ducked behind a garbage can lying on its side in the street. The gun was warming up to fire again.

"Are you okay?" Kay asked as she and Jericho tried to lift the bike up.

"Yeah, just a little winded," Mabel answered, she moved to help push the bike off, but stopped as she saw the rifle warming up, it was aimed back at her, "get out of the way, the rifle's going to fire."

Jericho stopped helping and looked back seeing the individual aiming at Mabel. Without a second thought to his fear, Jericho charged at the wielder, while throwing his rock lights. The rifle wielder changed their target and fired at Jericho. The blue beam struck Jericho on his shoulder. It caused his armor to explode, and the impact threw him into the air. He landed hard on the ground with his right side of his body exposed. Blood could be seen coming from a bad wound on his shoulder.

"Jericho!" Kay screamed, she left Mabel under the bike.

Baylor and Will jumped down from the container and rushed over to their friends. The people on the container continued to fire at the rifle wielder, as the wielder went back behind the garbage can. Baylor and Will lifted the bike off of Mabel with her pushing against it. They helped her up before running over to their wounded teammate.

Jericho wasn't moving. Kay disconnected her bracelets and the armor on her hands. She pressed her exposed hands onto Jericho's wound.

The rifle wielder prepared to fire at the group again, but this time the wielder was hit by a light blast from the container's top, and the rifle was turned off.

# Chapter 24

**Holding Cells, October 13, 2090 – 9:11 a.m.**

Codie could hear the fighting going on in the street, and fear was rising within him. The strange sounds of the weaponized lasers had reached his ears, and now he wanted to be out with his community helping. He was left alone in the cells, for everyone was trying to work on getting out of the station, and from the yelling, he could tell that the semi-trucks were keeping everyone in, as well as the back door being jammed from the outside.

The sound of a vehicle crashing outside made Codie rush to the cell window and looked out. He could barely see down the alley, but there were parts of a motorcycle scattered down it. Codie stepped away from the window and shook his head; he didn't want to wait anymore.

Codie wasn't handcuffed anymore, so he reached up and took his hair out from the ponytail it had been pulled back into. He took out lock picking tools that had been concealed by the hair tie. They had taken the items from his pockets and his leather jacket, but they hadn't checked his hair.

He started working on the holding cell lock. The stubborn lock wouldn't move the way he wanted it to, and his frustration was growing inside.

After failing for the third time, Codie smacked the lock with his fist causing his lock picking tools to fall out of the lock and onto the ground on the other side of the bars.

"Oh crap," Codie mumbled to himself.

He got down on his hands and knees and started reaching for the picks. His reach was just barely touching the small tools. They twisted on the hard floor, but he pressed his fingers hard on the ends of the picks and dragged them across the floor.

Picking them up, Codie started working on the lock again. He calmed his anger and fear inside and focused on the metal pins. He could feel them move as he shifted the picks inside. When suddenly a click brought a little joy, as the door swung open after being pushing on.

Codie was freed from the holding cell, and he almost wanted to jump for joy at achieving his freedom. But he didn't let himself celebrate as the sounds from the battle going on outside were getting louder.

He ran from his cell and to the desk at the end of the room. Opening one of the drawers, he found his leather jacket and items from his pockets. Pulling on his jacket, Codie opened the plastic baggy that contained his stuff. There was gum, a phone, and a wallet.

The gum and wallet weren't as important as the phone. He had modified it to hold the virus inside, if it had been accidentally turned on it could have affected everything in the building and nothing outside.

He grabbed his items and ran from the room.

**Police Station – 9:19 a.m.**

Codie ran into the main room of the station, where all the detective desks were, and looked around the room. It was complete chaos as people were making phone calls, running around, and trying to figure out what was going on. No one noticed him, and he wasn't looking for anyone specific but the stairwell. He needed to get to the roof, but he wasn't sure where the stairs were in the building.

Codie worked his way through the chaotic crowd of officers and detectives, as he went down a hallway. His eyes searched the doors and rooms for any sign of what he needed, which is why he didn't notice Detective Shepard as he bumped into her.

"Hey, watch it," she said to him.

The two of them locked eyes, before realizing who they ran into.

"Crap," Codie ran down the hall and back into the chaotic crowd.

Shepard chased after him, "how'd you get out?!"

The two of them went back into the detective area. Codie tripped and fell to the floor, Shepard didn't see him fall and ran past. Codie watched her run from his spot before standing up and backing away from her. She ran into a different room. And he thought he was free, but it didn't take long for Shepard to realize he wasn't in the room she had entered.

She came back into the detective room just to see Codie run down a different hallway, "stop!"

Shepard charged after him, and this time she was making sure she didn't past him again. The two of them rushed through the station like they were mice trying to reach the end of a maze. No one noticed their pursuit, as the fighting outside distracted everyone.

Codie slammed into a door, that was suddenly closed in his face, and he staggered back. Shepard took the opportunity to tackle the dazed man. They both smashed to the floor and struggled against each other.

"Let me go," Codie pushed against Shepard.

"No, you aren't getting away," Shepard had a strong grip on his jacket.

"I'm not trying to get away, I'm trying to help," Codie tried to stand up but was pulled back to the ground by Shepard.

"Right," Shepard said sarcastically.

Codie wiggled in Shepard's grasp and finally was able to get away as he took his jacket off. Shepard was left holding the jacket on the ground, as he ran down the hallway.

"You turd!" Shepard yelled at him.

She stood up and started chasing him again through the police station. This time the chase felt more like a cat and mouse, than two mice in a maze.

**Stairwell – 9:27 a.m.**

The door to the stairwell banged open as Codie stood in the doorway out of breath, "finally."

He started running up the stairs at a weaker pace. After going up a couple of steps, Shepard banged the door open too as she appeared in the doorway just as out of breath as Codie.

"Stop!" Shepard ordered, she pulled her gun from an ankle holster.

Codie heard the click of the gun and stopped going up the stairs, he turned around slowly and faced the Detective.

"Please," he pled, "I need to get to the roof. My friends are fighting the battle, and I don't want them to get hurt."

"Your friends, ha, so you admit that you are part of the attacks," Shepard's breath was still labored.

"No, my friends are the ones defending the station," Codie corrected, his feet shifted as he started working on a plan to get away from Shepard.

"Defending the station! There's a semi-truck crashed into the front of the building," Shepard shook her head, "you call that defending?!"

Codie didn't answer as he flipped one of his shoes at Shepard to distract her, as he ran up the last few steps of the stairs. Shepard fired her gun at the sudden movement, and the bullet bounced around the stairwell before slamming into a wall. She fell but got back up quickly. She aimed her gun just as Codie reached the door to the roof and fired. The bullet zipped through the air and into Codie's right leg.

"Crap," Codie fell back from the door and on to the steps below it.

He held his bleeding leg. The bullet had gone through the back of his calf but didn't break any bones. Shepard pointed her gun at him as she walked up the stairs slowly.

"Now you won't be able to run," she said.

"I'm not running," Codie said through gritted teeth, "I'm trying to stop the fighting. You may think I'm the enemy, but I'm the only ally you've got right now."

"Ally?" Shepard tilted her head, "that's not what I've seen."

Codie gave her a defiant look, "then you better put on some glasses because that's the truth."

Codie took his good leg and kicked Shepard in the stomach. He sent her rolling down the steps. She slammed into the wall at the bottom of the stairs.

Codie stood up on his good leg and hopped outside to the roof. Shepard sat up from the ground and touched her lip. A cut was on her bottom lip.

"That creep," Shepard picked her gun up and ran up the stairs after Codie.

**Police Roof – 9:34 a.m.**

Codie limped onto the roof, leaving a bloody trail behind him, and made his way to the edge so he could see what was going on. Reaching the edge of the roof his eyes saw the chaos going on in the street. Several motorcycles had been destroyed, and there were armored people from both sides on the ground not moving. He saw that there was a group forming of injured people's whose armors were destroyed, they were crouched behind several motorcycle parts to protect them from the fight. Most of individuals behind the motorcycle parts were bleeding in the group. The sounds of metal scraping against metal echoed across the street, as people fought with their fists.

Codie couldn't distinguish who was who fighting on the battlefield. All he knew was the yellow side was his side, and that the sea of multiple colors wasn't part of his community anymore. Shaking his head, Codie patted his pockets before digging into them to get his phone out.

"Don't move!" Shepard ordered from behind him.

Codie's hand was still in his pocket as he stopped moving, his phone needed to get out of his pocket so he could use it.

"Turn around slowly!" Shepard ordered.

Codie turned around slowly and faced the detective, her hair was messed up, and her lip was swelling.

"Now let me see your hands!" she pointed her gun at him.

Codie pulled out his phone and held his hands up.

"What's in your hand?!" Shepard was becoming agitated.

"A phone," Codie answered.

"Put the phone down!" Shepard stepped closer to him.

Codie slowly put the phone down and stood back up, "please, stop."

Shepard didn't listen to him, "turn around with your hands on your head!"

Codie did as he was told. Shepard walked up behind him with her gun still pointed at his back, but she put it away as handcuffs came out from her pocket.

Codie didn't wait for one more second and grabbed her hand, and he twisted it. He pushed her to the ground where he sat on top of her.

"Holy crap, get off me!" she ordered.

Codie sat on top of her like he would a sibling, "I'll get off, just give me a second."

He reached over and grabbed his phone, turning on the device he tapped a few things on the screen, before releasing the virus. Within seconds of its release, the sounds from the battlefield died down as the suits and motorcycles lost their power.

"What did you do?" Shepard asked.

Codie stared down at her, "well, I made a virus just for my community, I tried to make it so it would only affect the other side, but that didn't work. It should have stopped all the power from the suits and bikes."

**Palaco City – 9:38 a.m.**

All the lights coming from the armor and motorcycles went off, as it all lost power. It caused the fighting in the street to stop. The Vital Era team was behind the motorcycle parts barrier that had been built up to protect the injured from the battle.

Jericho was laying on the ground next to others who had been hit by a weaponized laser. His wound had stopped bleeding, and he had regained consciousness. Kay's helmet was off as she sat on the ground with his head in her lap. His helmet had been removed so he could breathe better.

Baylor, Will, and Mabel all stood around them, keeping watch during the fight. As their armored powered down, they removed their helmets. Their faces were covered in sweat.

"Codie was able to do it!" Will cheered.

Baylor nodded his head but remained silent. He still felt tense. Mabel looked around at the area and saw that almost everyone was either sitting down or taking off armor. Though their armor still protected them, the will to fight faded with the power. But her eye caught someone who started to run away.

Mabel took the opportunity to run after the armored individual. She caught up to the person and tackled them to the ground. Baylor had followed her after seeing her bolt and stood to watch as Mabel turned the individual over. She unclicked the helmet and pulled it off. Andrew, the leader of the Camo team, was under the helmet.

"Get off me," he squirmed.

Mabel held him tight, "why did you do this?!"

Andrew stared up at her, "because we thought we could win…we were told we could win. And that it was the only way to get back what we lost."

Mabel pressed harder against him, "and who told you that?"

Andrew spat into Mabel's face, and she wiped it off with the back of her hand.

"You better answer her," Baylor threatened.

"It was Joi," someone else answered.

Baylor and Mabel looked up and saw Winfred, a member of Codie's team the Rooks, standing in front of them with his helmet off.

"How do you know that?" Mabel asked she didn't let up on Andrew.

"While you were working on getting ready for this battle, Codie had his team go through the records on Joi," Winfred paused for a moment, "we found that she had been talking to the police. And after going through footage of the races, that she had been sabotaging games."

"That can't be," Mabel stood up.

Andrew tried to get up and get away, but Baylor placed a foot on his chest and kept him in place.

Winfred looked at his hands, "Codie has her being tracked now by her phone, if you want answers you better go with him to get her."

# Chapter 25

Codie stretched his arms and sighed with relief as the fighting stopped.

"Can you get off of me?" Shepard asked from underneath him.

He still sat on her like a big brother. Codie looked down at the Detective and smiled at her. She frowned at him.

"I would, but you're just going to arrest me," Codie looked up at the sky, "and I still need to do one more thing, then you can have me."

"One more thing," Shepard looked at him over her shoulder, "and what would that be?"

Before Codie could respond, Mabel climbed over the roof's edge. She landed on her back after reaching the roof. Her brown hair was very messed up, and sweat still covered her face. Mabel shook her head and stood up. Her armor had scrapes and dents from the fight.

"Hey Mabella," Codie greeted.

Shepard looked at her, "so you are part of the gang. I knew I was right."

Mabel gave Shepard a funny look as she saw Codie sitting on her, but didn't say anything as she walked over to Codie. Her face became very solemn.

"Winfred just told me about Joi," Mabel informed him.

Codie grew serious, "oh, well I guess that was going to come out. I was planning on going and getting her, but the Detective here shot me in the leg so I can't get away from her."

"Because you need to go to jail," Shepard wiggled, but still couldn't get free of Codie.

Mabel shook her head, "I want to go with you. I want to know why she turned on us."

Codie nodded slowly, "okay, but I don't think we are going to get an answer we can like. We tracked her phone, and she has been in the same place for the whole morning."

Mabel walked back to the edge of the roof and looked over, "hey, can one of you help us up here. Codie's sitting on Detective Shepard, so we need someone to take his spot."

Will and Kassidy both climbed over the roof's edge and stood on top of the building. Kassidy walked over to Codie, while Will stayed by Mabel.

"They've taken the wounded to the hospital. Kay went with Jericho," Will informed Mabel and Codie.

"Were any of the wounds bad?" Codie asked.

Will shook his head, "they were painful and sudden, but everyone should be fine."

Kassidy sat down on Shepard, with a small disagreement from Shepard, and Codie stood up with Mabel and Will helping him.

"Baylor is getting a car," Will told them.

"Okay," Mabel answered, "Will, would you stay here and make sure that everyone is taken care of?"

Will agreed, "yes, please be careful."

**Penguin and Sparrow Intersection – 10:12 a.m.**

Codie was lowered down from the police station roof with the help of Will and Mabel, he settled on the container's top and collapsed. His leg was still bleeding, but the flow of blood had slowed. Mabel jumped down from the roof and landed next to him. She helped him up again, and the two of them walked to the end of the container and started going down the semi-truck's front. They could hear people still panicking inside the station.

Winfred and Gayla, members of Codie's team the Rooks, came over and helped him get down off the vehicle. They looked happy to see their leader alive.

"Firemen and paramedics are on their way," Winfred informed.

"And we are keeping everyone here," Gayla said, "so we all can face our responsibilities together."

"Okay, Mabella is going to go with me to get Joi," Codie gave his two teammates hugs, "then we will return."

They said their goodbyes and walked down the street, to a car waiting among the rubble from the motorcycles and armor. Baylor was sitting in the driver's seat, waiting for the two of them. People were sitting on the sidewalks; most had their helmets off while they were trying to understand what was going to happen next.

There were a few individuals who had tried to run away, but no one let them get away. Not even their side was letting them get away with it. Those individuals had their whole armor removed, and were tied down by ropes, while someone kept watch over them.

Codie got into the passenger's side seat of the car, and Mabel started removing her armor so she could get into the vehicle. Baylor had already removed his own and placed it in the trunk.

Baylor looked at Codie's leg, "you should put something on that."

"Yeah I know," Codie touched the wound.

Mabel finished removing her armor and placed her gear in the trunk with Baylor's, she sat down in the backseat of the car, and pulled her belt out from her jeans and handed it to Codie, "here put this just above your knee to stop the bleeding."

Codie took the belt, "thanks."

Codie put the belt above his knee and tightened it up. Mabel waited for their destination to be revealed.

"So, where do you we need to go?" Baylor asked.

"Do you know where Fox Grove Graveyard is?" Codie asked.

"No," Baylor answered.

"Well, that's where we need to go," Codie leaned back into his seat, "but don't worry, I'll guide you there. Just try and get to the Bayside Point section of the city, it's going to be a long drive."

For the first few minutes, the small group drove in silence as they went through the city looking for Joi. But the questions bubbling inside of Mabel's mind didn't want to stay silent anymore.

"How did you know it was Joi?" Mabel asked Codie.

Codie let a sigh out, "well, there were a few reasons."

"Okay," Mabel coaxed him on.

"One of the first times I remember was when we had that big raid from the police," Codie paused, "when Felix died."

"I remember," Mabel whispered.

"Well, she wasn't anywhere to be found," Codie started his explanation, "she didn't even go to the meetup point for our team. I think she thought we would be caught. Because the police were stationed on the street, we usually met on."

Mabel and Baylor remained silent as Codie continued to tell of the betrayal that had happened.

"The next time something came up, is when your team was taken to the police station the first time," Codie continued to explain, "she called me.

And I'm pretty sure that she called me before you got to the police station or you had just barely arrived."

"Why would she target us? I thought she liked us," Mabel asked Codie, "I mean I don't remember ever offending her."

Codie shook his head, "it wasn't really about you Mabella. She targeted your team because she thought I would have turned myself in to save you from the consequences."

"Oh," Mabel mumbled.

"And the last thing that confirmed it for me," Codie sighed, "was when I hacked into the police station and loaded the pictures they had. Going through several of them, I realize Joi wasn't in any of them, even though I remember her being there. The pictures had dates on them, so there wasn't any way I was confused about it. And they focused on our teams specifically."

Baylor looked at Codie, "that pushed you over the edge. You suddenly knew it was her by that?"

Codie shook his head again, "I started investigating after that. I had Winfred, Gayla, and Lali started digging into Joi's records. We even started going through our pictures and videos. That's when we started finding out who was messing with gear and with people. She has been doing this since the end of your school year last year."

"Really?" Mabel couldn't believe it.

Codie continued with his tale, "and then we got into her phone records and found the number of Detective Shepard. She had started talking with Shepard during the summer."

"I just can't believe that," Mabel shook her head, "Joi helped form this community, why would she tear it down?"

"Well," Codie looked down at his own hands, "we have a theory, and it's not a happy one."

**Fox Grove Graveyard – 10:57 a.m.**

Baylor parked the car, and they looked at the Fox Grove Graveyard that was around them. The graveyard was very clean and had dark green grass everywhere. The trees were still young, but they looked like they were growing strong. It was a very nice place, people who came there could find peace as they viewed loved ones.

"Baylor, do you mind staying here?" Codie asked.

"No, I don't mind," Baylor answered.

Codie and Mabel exited the car, and both turned to the east side of the graveyard. Baylor stayed seated in the vehicle. The two of them left the small road, that went down the middle of the place, and walked onto the grass and among the headstones. They had both been to this graveyard before, but it had been almost a year ago.

They walked silently up a small hill, Mabel helped Codie walk with his wounded leg, and finally, they saw Joi. She had a black dress and purple silk jacket on, as she sat at a grave crying. She wept uncontrollably. There didn't seem to be any room for any other emotion.

Codie and Mabel walked slowly and quietly up to her until they could see the name on the headstone. Gary Newman was the name written on it. The young man that Mabel had seen die in front of her last Christmas.

Codie sat down next to Joi, "Joi."

He put his hand on her shoulder, and she jumped. She hadn't noticed them approach. She looked at both of them and noticed Codie's wound that still bled slightly.

Shaking her head, Joi cried, "I'm so sorry…I didn't want anyone to get hurt!"

Joi placed her head in her hands and continued to wail. Mabel walked over and sat down next to Joi on her other side. Mabel didn't know what to do or say to the crying woman. Her anger towards her died down upon seeing her sob.

"Joi, why?" Mabel whispered.

Joi looked up from her hands with tears flowing down her face, "because I thought it would stop us...Gary was going to propose to me, Hal gave me the ring Gary had bought for me...After that, I didn't want to be in the games anymore...I didn't want anyone to be in the games anymore...I just wanted it all to stop!"

Joi shook her head, Codie put his arm around Joi and pulled her into an embrace as she continued to sob. Tears formed in Mabel's eyes as she leaned over and put her arm around the two of them. They all sat there, staring at Gary's grave. Each remembering the night he died differently.

"I didn't know," Codie whispered.

**Bayside Point – 11:18 a.m.**

Baylor drove the car through Bayside Point. He was driving back to the police station. Codie, Mabel, and Joi were in the car as well. Codie sat in the backseat with Joi, who still sobbed, and Mabel sat in the passenger seat in front.  Mabel turned in her seat to face Codie.

"What are we going to do now?" she asked.

Codie looked out the car window, "we are going to turn ourselves in."

Mabel turned her head back to looking out the front of the car, "and what do you think will happen to us?"

"Well," Codie started guessing, "I would think we will all be charged with assault and a terrorist attack.  We did put the city into a panic, and our community did attack the police station."

"But not all of us did that?" Baylor pointed out.

"True," Codie rubbed the back of his neck, "maybe we will be able to work out a deal.  I mean I know there's going to be several fines, but we should be able to pay them and for the damages caused.  Hopefully, that will help."

"What about the games?" Mabel whispered her question, "are we done?"

"No," Codie answered promptly.

Joi looked at him with fear in her red eyes. He smiled and patted her hand.

"Don't worry Joi, the games we all knew are gone," Codie comforted her, "but Mabel found an old gym. And I do believe we can make our community there."

"What will the old gym do?" Joi asked.

"It will keep us off the street and safe," Codie explained, "and hopefully make the games legal."

"Really?" Mabel snorted, "I'm pretty sure we are all going to jail. I don't think there will be anyone left to see the games much less be in them anymore."

"That could be true," Codie agreed, "but we might as well hope for the best because thinking of the worst will only make it harder to do the right thing."

Baylor smiled to himself, "that's a funny way to look at it."

They continued to drive through Bayside Point until they got to the next section of the city. They didn't rush over to the police station, but they didn't drag their feet either. Their family and friends were still there, and no one wanted to leave them to take the fall. Though this community had been torn down, there still was a feeling of friendship among them even though some of the people didn't want to be a part of it anymore.

But it wasn't the end, and Codie was hoping he could still get another chance to make his games work.

# Chapter 26

**Police Station, October 13, 2090 – 11:49 a.m.**

Baylor drove the car up to the front of the police station. The semi-trucks were removed from the front entrance to the building, and the damage could be seen. Pieces of the building had fallen from the structure, and there were no longer any doors. It was just a big hole with people walking through it.

"We are going to pay for that," Mabel mumbled.

Baylor parked the car in front of the damaged building, and the four of them got out of the vehicle. Codie walked around the car to Joi; he escorted her up the steps of the station. Mabel walked over and stood by Baylor. The two of them looked at the building.

"How do you think Jericho is doing?" Baylor asked.

"He's probably doing good," Mabel grabbed Baylor's hand and squeezed it, "Kay is with him, so don't worry. She's going to watch him like a hawk."

Baylor nodded, "I'm glad she's there."

"Should we go in?" Mabel asked, she turned her attention to Baylor.

Baylor nodded again. The two of them walked up the steps of the police station and went inside the building. The entire place was full of people. Its hallways were jammed with officers and people from the Draconis community. Everyone had removed their armor, so there wasn't any threat of violence from them.

Baylor and Mabel made it to the main room of the station and saw Codie and Joi standing by Detective Shepard's desk. Shepard stood by her desk while yelling orders across the room as officers led some people away in handcuffs. Will was sitting at her desk working on her computer. They walked over to the group. Shepard saw them and pointed for them to stand by Codie and Joi.

Baylor and Mabel obeyed and stood by Codie. Shepard continued to give orders, while Will worked on her computer.

"So what are the damages?" Mabel whispered to Codie.

"Don't know," Codie whispered back.

Shepard finally stopped yelling and turned her attention back to the four individuals standing by her desk. She eyed each of them with great suspicion.

"Well, I'm glad the four of you came back," she said to them.

"I'm shocked you don't have us in handcuffs," Codie pointed out.

Shepard chuckled, "I was going to put you in handcuffs, but Wilt here made a deal on your behalf."

They all looked at Will, who still hadn't looked away from the computer.

"And what deal is that?" Mabel asked.

Shepard put a hand on her hip as she started to explain, "he has promised to upgrade our system network so it can't be hacked anymore, that all damages will be paid in full, that those who attacked the first time will be named and evidence will be given on them, and the games will no longer exist. But with all that, you Codie Wright are still going to jail."

Codie rubbed the back of his neck, "I thought that would be the case, do you know how long?"

Shepard sighed, "Wilt got it down to three months."

**Coloris Lapides, October 17, 2090 – 4:23 p.m.**

Mabel, Jericho, Will, Baylor, and Kay walked around the old Coloris Lapides gym. The entire building still smelled, and dust was on everything. The five of them had been given permission to leave school to visit the gym after they explained everything to Denzil. Jericho's shoulder was in a sling, so he wouldn't move it while the shoulder healed. He sat on the trunk that had been dragged in. Kay sat next to him. Will had a broom and was making a pile of dirt, while Baylor held a dustpan. Mabel was working on blueprints of how the place was going to change.

"So how is Codie holding up?" Kay asked Mabel.

Mabel looked up from her papers, "well they put him in a minimum security prison, so he can't complain. He does get a lot of visitors from the games."

"That's good, but I don't know what we will do without him," Kay commented.

"Why are we even here?" Jericho asked, "isn't the community done?"

Will stopped sweeping, "it is. But we are going to make a new one."

"Really?" Baylor asked.

Mabel smiled, "yup."

"But doesn't that go against what we agreed to with the police?" Jericho pointed out.

"We aren't going to be on the streets this time," Will explained, "we are going to do it legally. We will get permission from the city before we form anything else, and this gym is going to be where we do it now."

"Wow," Baylor commented, "will the old community agree to it?"

Kay snorted, "they will have nowhere else to go if they want to continue."

Mabel went back to drawing, as the room fell silent. Will started sweeping again, while Baylor waited for the pile of dirt to grow bigger. A thought entered Jericho's head as everyone went back to work.

"How are you going to pay for this? All the money we had went to the fines for the city," Jericho asked.

Kay smiled at him, "we are using Codie's money."

"Codie has money?" Jericho inquired.

"Well, to put in poker terms, he was the house," Kay said, "you do realize people placed bets on the games, right?"

Jericho shook his head, "no I didn't realize that. Is that how you all made your money?"

"Okay we didn't make any bets, but that is how the Draconis games did," Will chimed in.

"And is that how you plan to continue to make your money?" Jericho looked at Mabel.

Mabel stopped drawing again, "no, once we get up and running, we are going to run this like a sport. You'll need to pay to get a ticket. And betting will be banned."

# Epilogue

Mabel and Will walked into Lee Salvage Yard. The place had several workers going about their business, getting random pieces of metal ready to be smelted. Will watched the workers with fascination, he loved to see big pieces of metal be melted down. It made him excited.

The two of them walked over to a building in the middle of the yard and knocked on the door. A young woman opened the door and looked at the two high schoolers.

"Go back to school!" she yelled at them.

Mabel put her foot in the door so she couldn't slam it on them, "we have an appointment."

"Really?" the young woman sneered, "and what name would it be under?"

"Overton," Mabel answered calmly.

"Stay here," the woman left the door, after a few seconds she walked back, "okay you can come inside."

Mabel and Will entered the building; the young woman pointed to a couple of seats they could take, while she walked into an office. They took the seats and waited for a minute before the woman came back.

"Mr. Naylor will see you now," she pointed to the office she had come from.

They stood up from the chairs and walked into the office. A middle-aged man sat behind a desk. He had a t-shirt and jeans on and looked like he would rather be in the yard than behind the desk. He stood up and shook Mabel and Will's hands.

"Thank you for coming, I'm Mr. Naylor," he introduced himself, "please sit down."

Mr. Naylor sat down in his seat, while Mabel and Will sat down in seats in front of the desk.

"Thank you for seeing us," Mabel said.

"Your offer was one of great interest," Mr. Naylor smiled at the two of them, "so I felt I must find out if it was true or not."

"It is," Mabel confirmed, "we have seventeen metal containers."

Mr. Naylor inquired, "can I ask you where you got them?"

Mabel smiled at him, "we bought them from a vendor three years ago. They were no longer usable for cargo ships."

"Okay," Mr. Naylor made a funny face, "and why would you need seventeen metal containers in the first place?"

"They were for the Draconis Games," Mabel answered honestly.

Mr. Naylor nodded slowly, "the gang…well, I guess being disbanded you no longer need them anymore."

"Right," Mabel smiled but didn't correct him, "we just need to get rid of them, how much will you offer?"

Mr. Naylor rubbed his chin, "how about a thousand dollars for each of them?"

"Sounds good," Mabel agreed.

**Police Station, March 3, 2091 – 2:32 p.m.**

The police station had been rebuilt after the attack. It no longer looked like a semi-truck had crashed into it. The whole building looked normal. Codie thought it looked nice as he looked at it from the sidewalk. He hadn't seen it for a couple of months, so it was funny to see it looking like it did before the truck slammed into it. Codie wore his usual outfit with his leather jacket over his t-shirt. He didn't look like he had spent time in jail, even though he had been inside for three months and two weeks.

Codie walked up the steps of the buildings and went inside. Everything was calm as he walked up to the front desk. The secretary looked up from his computer.

"How can I help you?" he asked.

"I was hoping I could see Detective Shepard for a moment?" Codie inquired.

"Let me check to see if she is here?" the secretary picked up a phone and dialed an extension. After a couple of seconds, the line on the other side came alive, "hello Detective there is a young man here to see you…what is your name sir?"

"Codie Wright," Codie answered promptly.

The secretary gave him a weird look, "Codie Wright…okay."

The secretary hung up the phone, "she will be right out."

Codie waited at the desk for her. He continued to get looks from the secretary, but he didn't mind it. Shepard walked into the entrance area briskly. She wore a plain t-shirt and jeans with a leather jacket on. She almost looked like Codie's twin sister.

"Nice outfit," Codie smiled.

"Thanks," Shepard smirked at him, "I see you were finally released. Caused any trouble yet?"

Codie shook his head, "no, but I did come to show you something I have done."

Codie took out a piece of paper from his back pocket and handed it to Shepard. She took it and unfolded the paper. She read what was written on it.

"No crap," she smiled at him, "you've become legal…how did you get a permit like this?"

Shepard handed the paper back, and Codie put it away.

"It wasn't easy. A friend of mine had to wait a month to get it from the county office," Codie explained.

"Wow, so you are going to go through with the games after all that has happened?" Shepard asked.

"Yeah, we didn't mean for it to go sideways, but it still means a lot to us," Codie said, "but this time we want the police to know that we respect the laws and don't want to break any."

"Good luck with that," Shepard smirked again.

Codie smiled at her, "so I am here to personally invite you to the grand opening of the Draconis Games."

Codie handed her a ticket, "we hope to see you there."

**Coloris Lapides, March 5, 2091 – 6:46 p.m.**

The old Coloris Lapides gym didn't look anything like it used to. The outside had been painted black, with lines of reflective paint going across the building like lines on a circuit board. Whenever lights from cars would hit it, yellow would be reflected back. All the windows had been replaced, and lights glowed from within as the night sky covered the city.

Once inside, the true changes could be seen. The front entrance had been cleaned up with black paint on the walls and black tile instead of carpet, and now a desk at the front greeted people. It also barred people from entering without a ticket that could be purchased at the front desk as well.

After purchasing a ticket, you could enter the stadium. The bleachers were a story off the main floor, so they hovered above the playing field that had been built on the first floor. The playing field was big, there was a racetrack that went around, that let the modified motorcycles race. There was a center area where players could be participating in a match between teams. Metal objects were placed on the platform so players could hide behind them during the games.

It had taken months to fix the old gym to the new stadium it was, but the effort had paid off. People were drawn to the building; they wanted to see what was inside or wanted to see the gang that had terrorized their city. Either way, they went inside to be surprised.

Mabel and Kassidy were at the front desk, greeting people and giving them tickets. Mabel and her team had been given permission by the school and their parents to work at the Draconis Games, as real-life experience. They also had suffered a lot of detention over the last few months because of the school absences.

Kassidy sat at the front desk talking to the people who came in, while Mabel was counting tickets out to those who purchased them. Their grand opening was going well, and people liked what they saw.

Detective Shepard walked through the crowded doors and up to the desk. She butted in line because her ticket was already in her hand.

"Mabella Overton," Shepard greeted.

Mabel looked up from counting tickets and smiled as she realized it was the Detective, "Detective Shepard, I'm glad you came."

"Well I had to see this place for myself, and make sure you're not breaking any laws this time," Shepard joked.

"There shouldn't be anything questionable happening here," Mabel confirmed.

"Are your friends and brother here?"

"Yeah, they're working behind the scenes tonight," Mabel informed.

"Well, maybe I will see them," Shepard nodded at Mabel and walked towards the stadium in the building.

## The End.

If you liked the story here, there are others to read. The next story that will be coming out is "Lost Miracle: Blood in the Water".

Also, if you want to keep up to date with what is happening, you can always visit the blog at **dragonphilosopher.com**. Where new stories are always posted.

# Lost Miracle: Blood in the Water

Summary:     "I'm not shocked," Terry frowned, "father didn't know what safety was, even when the secret service was there. Probably from his days in the military."

She continued to gaze upward, "what should we do?"

"Give up," he stated, "we never knew who he was fighting, and we could make a good life. And make our own decisions."

Mary looked at her brother and frowned, "you didn't read the last page."

Terry wrinkled his forehead and looked at the documents again. After several seconds of reading, he let another sigh out.

"The hero who killed Ian Young, who the government is supporting, is personally tracking down the Young family, for it is believed they aided and abetted him," Terry read aloud.

He looked up at his sister and sighed once again, "rats, I hate heroes."

www.ingramcontent.com/pod-product-compliance
Lightning Source LLC
Chambersburg PA
CBHW032021240626
47153CB00013B/1665